I0551690

"A Manifesto About Stalking

Patrick Hyland."

By Francis Nally

Choam Charity Publishing #003
Philadelphia, PA USA

ISBN-10: 0-9989203-2-0
ISBN-13: 978-0-9989203-2-0

First Edition,

Second Printing, 2018

Printed in the USA.
Cover design by Shelby Criswell
https://www.fiverr.com/shelbycriswell

Thank you Piss for the edits.

PRAISE FOR FRANCIS NALLY

"perhaps I'm a 'normie' then, because it is certainly not good enough for me." - Adam Parfrey

"lolol asian pill. idk man shit is crazy in general right now. wild times." - Sam Hyde

"The alt-right is atrocious and the fact that you're giving those morons oxygen is more than enough to dissuade me from appearing on your show." - Chris Korda

"[Francis Nally] embodies the harmonic whimsicality that Elliot Rodger might have realized, had he channeled his emotions more constructively and stuck to Asian chicks." - Brandon Adamson, author of *Beatnik Fascism*

"[Francis Nally] inherently understands the alt-right and alt-left are empty signifiers of the same collective – rudderless, underdeveloped males. *Almond Eyes, Baby Face* dares to envision a newly-grafted race, one willing to pick up arms for its survival. It is refreshing to see such dangerous thoughtcrime still being practiced in these ultra-puritanical times." - James Nulick, author of *Valencia*

"[Francis Nally], a true literary outsider, explores themes and ideas that are totally outside of what we're accustomed to expect from literary fiction. He is an absolute original and a unique voice in contemporary literature. Shake off your boring vanilla expectations and experience the world of Trip—if you dare!" - Casper, editor of fluland.com

"The leading Asian-Aryan Alt-Right intellectual of his generation." - Luke Ford

"Well, I like that it is good, clean writing, no literary pretension. Your own original manifesto on Asian girls, a subject I know little about. It would be too much work for me to critique, something I never like to do. For all I know, you could have a hit on your hands." - Josh Alan Friedman, author of *Black Cracker*

"[Francis Nally] is one of the more vital and interesting voice of the alt right and new counter culture. He has cross platform talents from pod-casting to video blogging and his new book form literary endeavors are well worth your time to take a look at." - Richard Wolstencroft

"Where I can support Asian-Aryanism fully and unequivocally, however, is in viewing Asians and white as having largely emerged under the same hyper-social evolutionary pressures, and to therefore see the problems facing whites as problems which already - and even more so in the future - are felt by Asians." - HAarlem VEnison

"For Matt. I believe in you. Just like the Talk Talk song. And for Aivy. You know why."

FOREWORD BY BRANDON ADAMSON

"Pilleater" was the moniker Francis Nally was using when I (virtually) met him through my casual involvement in co-hosting The Stark Truth podcast with Robert Stark. At the time, I assumed the name Pilleater was a reference to the popular "pill meme," (ie taking the red pill, the black pill, the iron pill etc) and that his usage of this particular handle was intended to signify that this "pill popper" was an individual who just couldn't help himself from indulging in chewable after chewable of the forbidden flavored "truth" tablets purportedly offered by the emerging alternative political scene. As usual, it turned out I was grossly overthinking it and "pilleater" was just an obscure reference to his ytmnd.com ("ytmnd" is an acronym for You're the Man Now Dog) profile username from 2009 and was a pun on the term "inkdrinker." So basically, I was way off. My only real understanding of him was that he was heavily promoting something called "Asian-Aryanism." Since I have never had much of an Asian fetish or any kind of fascination with Japanese culture (aside from buying a few anime VHS tapes back in 2004-2005 and watching Urusei Yatsura and Evangelion, which I was introduced to by a long gone ex-girlfriend named Brandie,) what Francis Nally saw in my ideas that he identified with was a complete mystery to me.

As I've come to discover over time though, the purveyors of the bizarre and avant-garde that linger on the outer rings of the political dissident sphere tend to gravitate toward one another, irrespective of ideological differences. Anyone that feels out of step with the frat boys, dwarven nationalists, and tradfags, and paroled members of prison gangs, inevitably finds themselves defacto cohorts in the miscellaneous crap pack.

If Francis is to be understood, it is first and foremost as an artist. He is an astonishingly creative individual, cranking out musical projects, novels and performance art videos at practically Warhol factory productivity levels. Even his most trivial endeavors take unlikely turns and hit you from multiple unexpected angles. His video review of Guillaume Faye's contemporary classic, *Archeofuturism*, is the perhaps most bizarre book review I've ever come across. Some might write it off as someone acting retarded online for lulz, but ultimately the review gets at some deeper, hidden truths in the process, subtle truths about how seriously we take biographies, descriptions, buzzwords and brands.

Like many politically inclined young men in the generation subsequent to mine, Francis Nally has always struck me as alien. He comes from a culture of seemingly confused, ideological tourists: incels and volcels and NEETS and creeps, all riding the memetic wave along the radioactive coastline. Over the past year or two, I have witnessed Francis Nally at times flirt with AltRight ideas, interviewing various white nationalist figures, even going so far as to attend rallies, such as that most infamous of gigs: the shindig in Charlottesville. I've also seen him disavow all of these things and the most of the figures associated with them. I've known Francis to explore and express support for manosphere, MGTOW and PUA communities while often heavily directing criticism toward those groups as well. To this day, I have no clue what his actual beliefs are. His one constant, unshakable ideological principle seems to be his attraction to Asian girls and advocacy of dating them. On this issue, he conducts himself with the focus of a serial killer with a laser-sighted crossbow.

Perhaps this book will provide the naked insight we've all been waiting for. Just who is Francis Nally? What sort of government does he think is ideal? What kind of society does he wish to live in, and whom would be allowed within its boundaries? Francis advocates for a kind of Eurasian futurism that is peculiarly plausible and in fact already emerging as a new aristocracy in some parts of the United States, such as Silicon Valley and Seattle. The pages that follow undoubtedly represent the most comprehensive and definitive articulation of Francis Nally's idiosyncratic vision that the world has ever seen. Believe me when I say there is enough substantive material in here to intrigue and alienate everyone. This book is part manifesto, part memoir and part pool orgy. So strip down, slip your best neon striped Speedo on and dive right in!

-B.A.
www.altleft.com
March, 2018

What is Asian-Aryanism?

"Asian-Aryanism" is a whimsical term to describe a movement of Asians, whites, and Eurasians that seek a peaceful and progressive community together, and further, to promote better race relations between the two parties and beyond. We want a future identity that is proud to be white, Asian, Eurasian, and "Asian-Aryan," all at the same time.

The word "Aryan" was chosen because it suggests a "supreme, master race." We do not advocate Nazism or any racist ideologies. Rather, we are a collective that is anti-SJW, red-pilled, and against the liberal establishment. The word "Aryan" is a playful term that might seem racist at first, but is quite the opposite.

Being racially mixed is a challenge for some. We see Eurasians/hapas as a part of a new, healthy identity. But we also want to retain the identities of all white and Asian civilizations. However, we are lost in a new identity that is defined as a post-Asian-American culture.

We are white men that prefer to be with Asian women, we are Asian men that like both white and Eurasian women, and we are Asian women that unapologetically like white men too. This new identity isn't any sort of white nationalism or Asian elitism. This is Asian-Aryanism.

9

Anyone you know who is married to an Asian woman or has Eurasian children, are Asian-Aryans. They need a new identity, and a community like us, to empower them and give them a new meaning in life.

Modern culture promotes a victim mentality that weakens Asian men and Eurasian people. It makes the white man scared and the Asian woman agitated. We prefer to be with white/asian/eurasian people like ourselves, and consider each one a brother and a sister.

The Asian-American community, and some hostile SJWs, will deem us as "racist." Times are changing. We have to move forward with a humorous, "race-play" brand of "Asian-Aryanism" in order to get the message across.

The best way to talk about racial issues is to joke around with our differences until we are comfortable and proud of those differences. Some of us want to believe that we are "created equally." But we believe that whites and Asians are the only true equals. Let's not convolute the message and say "everything is relative." We are a new group of people.

For the first time, Asians and whites are finding a peaceful bond together. This is a romance that no one wants you to know about. It's time to come out of the closet and work together as a group.   *1-10-17*

Aim for the Ace! / Shin Ace o Nerae! (1979)

I first saw the *Aim for the Ace!* (*Aim for the Best!* as it might be called) movie when I was a freshman in college. It was Valentine's Day, and the Japanese club thought it would be nice to play an ironic, so-called "avant-garde" film in the afternoon.

I was good friends with this blue-haired, Chinese-American girl named Sarah. She only dyed her hair blue because, well, that's what all the white girls did. She would rely solely on me for homework help. We had something going on. The fact that I was the only role model in the room made it seem like I would be a good white boyfriend. I was exactly the type she would gravitate towards. The alt-right would probably call this archetype, "the orbital, beta-male cuck."

I remember having lunch by myself as a hermit. And then she saw me. She waved, smiled, and came over to talk, as if she was a good friend I had known for a long time.

She said something like, "Do you want to see this really cool anime from the 1970s called Aim for the Ace?"

I remember saying something back, like "That sounds awesome!"

She sounded like some groovy mod-girl from the 1960s.

Young people love to play on this funky lingo to express their personalities. A fine mix of ignorance, naiveté, immaturity, confusion, and social pressure.

Sarah was a cutie. I would **have** considered her my girlfriend at the time. Often she would flirt with me by saying, "…I need you as a boyfriend today!" I really didn't know what she meant by that, other than she just wanted to have fun.

Being so young, I was too "autistic" to figure out her cues. Or even brave enough to ask her on a date. I could not distinguish between **a** friend and **a** potential lover. I would say "yes" to all her petty commands. I believed I was naturally meaningful to her.

Young people **always seek** others to do something for them. Sarah was that type. If **there was** any possible accusation that I was her boyfriend, she would outright deny it. I was too afraid to put our relationship in jeopardy.

Sarah, although Chinese, **associated** with anime and Japanese culture for the sake of belonging to an ambiguous "Asian" culture. A culture **obviously** made up by white people to categorize what they like. If she was to be a "normie," then she had to be a white one. That also meant picking up all the sarcastic, ironic, and typical hipster things young white people do.

And of course, she pretended to be an anime character as a way to attract white boys, like me.

We went to the movie together. Not hand in hand, but side **by** side.

I was sitting with her in a dark theater, a matinee show, about to watch a vintage anime about tennis.

You could say it was a date. She didn't have the words to express **this**. Maybe because she was too afraid to actually consider it one.

This movie was from 1979, and it was a very moving experience for me. **It was just me and the picture show** in the room together. I forgot about Sarah and the thirty other students. **I was** amazed at the watercolor-esque pictures and that old synthesizer soundtrack.

…And I thought it would be some kind of trashy emo stuff made in the last 10 years. I was wrong.

"Oka Hiromi, 15 years old," I clearly remember reading on the screen.

Hiromi is a high school student who balances her life as a student and as a tennis player. She and her friend Maki enjoy growing up together. Unfortunately, Hiromi is taught by a brutal coach, who secretly loves her. This love is very similar to what Sylvia Plath once said, "*every woman adores a fascist.*"

This movie is about Hiromi's transition from childhood to a future career. It is that typical "coming-of-age" film, **but also** a snapshot of life in Japan during the late 1970s.

Yuiko Mishima died in 1970. Mishima warned that a decade later, Japan would succumb to the Western powers of decadence and Stuff-White-People-Like culture. Japan must either defend itself or perish.

I believe anime in the 1990s was fully exploited. An apex of white interests finally took notice of Japanese culture. However, white people were never interested in Japanese pop art prior to the 1980s. *Aim for the Ace!* came right at the end of a forgotten decade.

The film is filled with technological things of the past. Arcades, movie theaters, bad glasses, the synth soundtrack, bad art decor… Things of the decaying 1970s and the rise of the 1980s.

Brandon Adamson over at **www.altleft.com** fantasizes about a white America that could return to a space-age

14

culture. Not much of an actual ideology, but the word "alt-left" is rather a classification of an artistic lifestyle. *Aim for the Ace!* could be compared as a Japanese, alt-left aesthetic piece of art.

I remember Sarah looking at me while I turned my head in different directions, trying to understand what was really going on. She thought it was just a cute movie to bond **over**. But I was serious about it.

The interaction between Hiromi and Maki is some of the best Japanese dialogue I have watched. Constantly, the film portrays the characters in social situations talking about everyday drama. The cutest part of the film is when both are off from work. The two naturally bond together in post-fascist Japan. We don't learn about them as characters, but rather, we learn about the current society of Japan.

…The bustling train, the old architecture, the strangers walking by. …I was paying close attention to all the details, not the plot, of the film.

My Japanese is very elementary. I can pick up words like a kid and can understand simple concepts. If you don't know the language, however, it's better to turn off the subtitles and watch the movie without it. The best art can be understood through a simple, universal, and ignorant language.

The movie was obviously made for young girls. Often kiddie excitement is attached to it, abandoning adults to enjoy the film (depending if this only applies to Japanese adults).

The life of these young Japanese is post-fascist. Day after day, test after test, obtaining all the knowledge of the world, and then using their bodies for competition. It's not an attitude based upon, "individual work effort," but a discipline among the Japanese people. Hiromi and Maki are happy with their lives, even though a normie white person might call their lifestyle, "national socialism."

To make things worse, there is even a classic love/hate relationship with the fascist coach, who rules over an entire tennis team of young girls.

It's domination. It's cruelty. …It's *fifty shades of grey*!

"Every woman adores a fascist."

And Hiromi slowly falls for the fascist coach! This is through sadomasochistic torture and ~~by~~ violent means. Not from her own consent, but by force. It reads like a classical tale by Mishima. This is exactly what disturbs the average white viewer: the thought that the Japanese are violent, innate fascist.

The film is unapologetic about discipline and work. Again, the reality of race between whites and Japanese. *Aim for The Ace!* is about traditional roles and society. It is the love of the Japanese spirit through tennis. No one is ever worthy, but the one who wins in the struggle.

I remember squinting my eyes taking every English subtitle **as** significant. I didn't laugh or show any emotion. The movie caught my attention **at** every second.

A good artsy movie exploits the camera. The characters in the film act like real **people**. I saw the film as a documentary instead. The plot is totally ambiguous. One scene could be about gossip, and then the **next could** have no purpose at all. Don't watch the movie for the story, just watch it as a moving art piece. It's an aesthetic and an emotion brought upon the viewer.

It **is** the perfect "stoner" movie, you could argue.

When the movie was over, I remember Sarah telling me to **stand** up with her. I didn't want to. I was still in my seat waiting for the movie to leave my consciousness. I didn't want to come back to reality.

Me and Sarah went out to eat after the film. All I remember was her saying, "it was cute." I disagreed.

The day after, I remember finding the film online and watching it again in my bed. I wanted to feel those deep neglected, emotions again ("feels" you might call **them**).

Four years later, I **still** remember the perfect Valentine's Day watching **of** *Aim for the Ace!* Life is aesthetically perfect in that film.

2-20-17

The Book of the Angel's Egg: Yoshitaka Amano and Gene Wolfe

The Anime Right is a spin-off of The Alt-Right, but has its own unique personality. There is an apparent influence from Eastern culture more than from Plato or Shakespeare. A 14/88er would argue against anime and be in favor for traditional figures like them.

Anime is quite controversial for the traditional Alt-Righter. But in no way is it "degenerate."

Jason Reza Jorjani in his book *Prometheus and Atlas* defends both *Akira* and *Neon Genesis Evangelion* as "premium animes," relating them to the philosophy of Martin Heidegger.

So how can there be this cross-over between anime and the Alt-Right? Do the Japanese even know of such a phenomenon?

We can begin with the concept that the Japanese are influenced from everything in western tradition, like Plato and Shakespeare. They chase after western art because it is supreme. The Japanese will then emulate an existing classical piece of art and then culturally appropriate it. I remember when I was little, *Akage no Anne* (1979) and *Sherlock Hound* (1984) would be playing on TV.

I liked the pretty pictures and could care less about the plot. However, take a closer examination, and realize both were based upon the European works of *Anne of Green Gables* and *Sherlock Holmes* respectively. The Japanese still look at the western world as being unapologetically successful and racially aware.

Unfortunately, they are naive when it comes to the Jewish Question or the demise of white people.

There is a cult piece of literature that the Alt-Right is unaware of. It is the very controversial and underground book series, *The Book of the New Sun* by Gene Wolfe. This isn't your typical science-fiction or fantasy novel. The title "New Sun," could be easily replaced with the word, "Black Sun."

The book series is often cited by comedians Sam Hyde and Charls Carroll under the Million Dollar Extreme Reddit as a reoccurring joke. Hyde is especially fond of the book for some reason. It's probably because it's too avant-garde for the Alt-Right to get. However, it's actually quite an easy book to enjoy once you start decrypting the scripture of the holy prophet, Severian.

New Sun has been compared to *The Lord of the Rings*. But why hasn't there been any media outreach for the series? It is because the book has been translated from some obscure language of the future, not intended for a normie audience. It requires the reader to observe than to engage. It is classical speculative fiction, par excellence.

A few years later, *Neuromancer* (1984) became a box office hit, and got more attention as a perverted "postmodern" dystopia, loved and advocated by our hostile elites (not to mention, the explicit love of being cucked over by the Japanese). It buried the rising success of the first part of The New Sun, *The Shadow of The Torturer* (1980).

Unlike Neuromancer, The New Sun is a work based upon a future beyond cyberpunk. Wolfe claims that he is the only person on this Earth with the skill to translate this alien work. Call The New Sun a "prophecy" rather than a science-fiction novel. Hypothetically, the angel Gabriel came into Wolfe's sleep and he was given an oracle vision of the far future. The same has happened in William Hope Hodgson's *The Night Land* (1912). Isaac Asimov wrote stories about robots to sell to pulp magazines, but Wolfe had a vision.

Now, Japanese fine artist Yoshitaka Amano was deeply influenced by The Book of the New Sun. In the mid-80s, before his work on *Vampire Hunter D*, Amano did the cover art for the official Japanese editions of all four books in the series. His art is "fearful" and decaying, just like "The

Dying Genre" itself (Wolfe's book should be synonymous with the genre).

At that same time in 1985, five years after The Shadow of the Torturer, we have Amano's first breakthrough film, *Angel's Egg* (1985).

I remember seeing Angel's Egg being advertised at my local art-house movie theater. However, I never had the chance to go. I was safe on my college campus and didn't feel like going outside as a loner. But to see this movie in theaters is an amazing experience! I regret not going.

The movie is Amano's mid-80s work on display. His prime. Everyone knows that "Amano" is now associated with the overrated video-games series, *Final Fantasy*. Just like how Akira Toriyama now means *Dragon Ball* and even *Dragon Quest*. Any hardcore fan should know that all of Amano's art before 1987 was influenced by Wolfe's vision in some way.

...Ok, I do like Ozuma (the orb of confusing art) and the final boss Necron that have both appeared in Final Fantasy 9 many years later. I'm not sure whether Amano had input into those designs.

The Japanese (translated into English) for Ozuma reads like this:

"The metaphysical being Ozma exists without form and is unknowable, untouchable, and unattainable. And it is indispensable. Those who recognize it will be forced to question existence, being, the gods, and themselves."[1]

…Sounds like Wolfe's work, yes?

Amano's art is heavily influenced from the works of H.R. Giger, Jean Giraud, and the art nouveau style of Aubrey Beardsley and Harry Clark. Mineo Maya's longest-running and gender-queer manga, *Patalliro!* surely has been read by Amano.

Watching Angel's Egg again, it certainly brings the viewer into a desolate world. A different reality unlike our own world. The same way Wolfe does with his work.

The Book of The New Sun is a long memoir by Severian, a Journeyman and prophet that foretells of a future society. Remember, "The Book" is not written in English, it's translated. The reader should passively engage the text and try to make up his own claims about how Wolfe presents the words. Severian's writing is supposed to be "in a tongue that has not yet achieved existence."

---

[1] Ozma's CollectaCard

23

As for Severian being, "an unreliable narrator," were Lao Tzu or Muhammed "unreliable" when they wrote their books?

For the purpose of word-play, I do believe that the bird-embryo thing in the first scene of Angel's Egg is actually a "*destrier,*" a giant horse-like monster from the future. Yes, it's a "bird" and not a horse of course, but the point is, that the setting is so far into the future, that humanity (*is it even called that?*) has lost the words to describe any original meaning.

Wolfe's translated words can have deeper meanings, like *fuligin* (darker than black). There can be archaic and obscure words. They are not invented up by the author, but revitalized from original words. Often so, words are suggestive rather than definitive (if the word 'horse' is used, it's doesn't exactly mean the animal, but something like it).

…Who is the master race in the future of The New Sun? They seem to be people known as the "Ascians." Possibly, The "Asians." Or what I like to call, "Asian-Aryanism." Wolfe has denied such a claim, but I don't care.

Amano and the Japanese would be open to the idea of a great civilization made up of European-Japanese. That one popular anime, *Shingeki no Kyojin*, is made up of fictional

"Asian-Aryan" people in a distant future. Half-White, Half-Japanese.

Watching Angel's Egg gives you a glimpse into a world of future people where there is a new race of people with alien technology and architect.

Remember Final Fantasy 7 and Cloud's Buster Sword? It reads very similar to Severian's Terminus Est, an overpowered sword of some sort. The unspeakable future of Angel's Egg and The New Sun also has feudal knights in surrealist landscapes.

The "Dying Earth" theme has been played again in the first Final Fantasy movie, *Final Fantasy: The Spirits Within* (2001). An underrated classic, the film imagines a world where the military tries to overthrow the Amano-esque science of the "Gaia." A very similar plot is written in Angel's Egg. The military and the oppressing forces of both films are stopped by a messiah.

Severian liberates the world with a "New Sun," ending the Kali Yuga and beginning a new golden age, where the Earth is green and beautiful again.

The male character in Angel's Egg could be Severian for all we know! Amano has drawn and played with Wolfe's characters many times in his own art prior to 1984. It's likely he would use those same character designs again in the movie.

There is also a Christian message in both Angel's Egg and in the New Sun. A cross appears in the movie, and that the egg can represent a metaphor as the birth of Jesus. Severian is a messiah for Pagan's that reject Christianity. Considering Wolfe's work as "Christian" is blasphemous. "The New Sun" in it's design is esoteric paganism. The Japanese have been obsessed with "the sun," as it is an emblem on their countries flag and represents the constant struggle of birth and death (like Jesus Christ).

The newer Japanese editions of The Book of The Sun feature art done by Takeshi Obata, who did the art for *Death Note*. From that perspective, The Book of The New Sun for the Japanese gives them strength in a dying, futuristic society.

Many who have read The Book of The New Sun agree Wolfe's vision is similar to that of Amano's vision in the video-game series Final Fantasy. I can't really explain Amano's art in my own words. But in Wolfe's word, it can. Wolfe has even said while translating Severian's language, "What the actual language may have been, I cannot say." (Appendix)

If you want to learn more about The Book of The New Sun, instead of reading the very first book, The Shadow of The

26

Torturer, I suggest picking up the *Lexicon Urthus* book which is a collection of lore from the series. It does a good job trying to explain the world to any normie.

The art of Yoshitaka Amano, along with the words of Gene Wolfe, leave the impression of a new cultural and political movement yet to come. The Anime Right should shift towards this avant-garde aesthetic while remaining faithful towards the Alt-Right message of manifesting destiny.

Now, as a warning about approaching Wolfe's work, Severian warns the reader:

"Here I pause, having carried you, reader, from gate to gate… If you wish to walk no farther with me, reader, I cannot blame you. It is no easy road."

3-9-17

Getting "The Anime Right" Out of The Alt-Right Bag

My mom was trying to tell me something about a recent outburst on TV.

"Did you see it yet? The politician's kid came in the room when he was live on TV! Not only that, but his wife is Korean! He is keeping his life a secret! A white man that is this big, influential politician, has an Asian wife! I think the wife is deliberately pushing the kids back in the room is because she wanted to get notoriety around the world that she is an Asian wife with a white husband!"

…Really?

And then there was that one time, a week ago, I found out that Based Stickman's wife was Asian too.

A small world we live in.

Dr. Robert E. Kelly, a diplomat and occasional columnist, had a blooper on a live BBC interview, when his little kids came walking in the room. And then that crazy tiger-mom came in and saved the day. Making the scene much worse.

Kelly said in a press conference, "...My real life punched through the fake cover I have created for television. ... There I am, in my suit... and reality burst in. ...The fallout for my academic credentials. ...I'm BBC Dad." (New York Times)

Saying this all in a professional manner, while his beautiful wife, Kim Jung-A, and his kids, Marion and James, stand up for him.

...I don't know any Asian kids named "Marion" and "James." Those are Eurasian names. Better yet, white names.

I thought about what my mom said. It's cute at first when the kids disturb his professionalism. However, there are few things that can get on a normie's nerves:

1. The crazy oriental mom. What is she going to do to her bastard kids in the other room? Punish them? Asians must be fish monsters!

2. "...He's got an Asian wife? What the hell man?! What is this guy into? He looks so normal!"

3. His face when he is closing his eyes. Pretending his wife and kids are not in the same room (pretending the Elephant is not there, his Asian wife).

These points make you wonder whether there is a giant conspiracy about what the WASP elites do in their private lives.

Do a majority of white professionals have Asian wives, and keep it a big secret?

The cat is out of the bag! Asian-Aryanism is real!

The WASP elite just pretend they are just like you, but have kids unlike themselves!

Now imagine where these kids are going to end up in twenty years. How powerful will they be? Will they end up like Elliot Rodger? Will this blooper mark their fame?

"Yeah, I was the kid in that video. Now let me into Harvard," James says to the admission.

They could have never stepped foot in the room, and Kelly would have continued his private life.

Now the public knows he's a race traitor! Right!? (They didn't say the same thing about Based Stickman, did they?)

What I learned from watching this blooper too, was that the Anime Right is actually getting out of the Alt-Right bag.

To be a Hollywood Nazi, you had to listen to Skrewdriver and say "Nigger" all the time. To be someone who is Alt-Right, you have to read The Right Stuff daily and be up to date on the meme war.

Well, what happened to those innocent guys that liked anime, played video-games, and had Asian girlfriends?

They had to cover up that "degenerate" stuff. They had to worship the "Aryan woman in the wheat field," just so they could be cool in front of their Discord friends. When it comes to IRL gatherings, The Anime Right isn't there.

We have to ask what Jared Taylor's favorite anime is and capitalize on it. We have to ask Greg Johnson, Mike Enoch, Richard Spencer, …All those figures you can think of on the Alt-Right, and then have a national Anime-Coming-Out-Day.

If Jared Taylor's favorite anime was *Doraemon* when he was growing up in Japan, let's make it a cultural meme. (All the hot Asian girls I know are swag'd out with Doraemon stuff).

31

The Anime Right is a scene where everyone comes out as a weeb on the Alt-Right. They are still afraid to show their pride with anime, and rather don a troll persona.

"This is about winning the troll war! Yeah! It's about pretending to be like weebs and then proselytizing every nerd to get on the Alt-Right!"

Yeah right.

We now know that Mr. Kelly's kids are Asian-Aryan. It was a big secret, until they came crawling over on live international TV. Now we all know what he's into.

Don't be afraid to be open about loving Asian culture. Schopenhauer and Nietzsche had great things to say about the culture of the orient. And the women too!

So what if you like anime? You probably wish life was like an anime.

There are some ramifications to that, of course. I had some quarrels with some posers on Twitter that are totally 14/88 and are white advocates, yet they seem to love pictures of blonde anime pagan girls or some white society done by an artist influenced by anime. I tell each and everyone one of them that they are "secretly into Asian-Aryanism." They will always rebut with a pathetic, "This has nothing to do with the Japanese! It's white people! Therefore, whites like me, naturally like it!"

…Just like that one time this Japanese-American complained to me on Twitter. She said, "Well, my husband is white, but why should that matter?" Problem solved! The answer is right in front of you! Things have never been so obvious.

People like to question what is real. You can't find innocent with the guilty. Everyone is guilty for loving anime. Don't try and make it seem so invisible.

Harvey Milk was an openly-gay American politician that won a seat in the public office of California. How did he go about winning in 1978? By telling the public that every gay person you knew was *not* a monster.

"Your veteran, the fireman, the baker, all of them are gay! What wonders gay people can do for society!"

The Alt-Right should be open about its love for Eastern culture. The Anime Right is a cat that came out of the bag of The Right Stuff's shitposting. Let the world know that we are into twee and cutesy stuff from the East, as well as some of that dank and edgy avant-garde stuff too.

As for Mr. Kelly and his kids: cats out of the bag too! The elites like Asian women!

3-16-17

The Meaning Behind *Spirit*

I woke up one morning after a traumatic dream about my senior year in college. I didn't have work that day, or I just didn't feel like committing time to it.

I had to check my Twitter and Facebook. In my Twitter feed, I found out about *You Are The Hero Vol. 2*. Should I spend my cash on that? I love Fighting Fantasy stuff. Great books.

Then it hit me.

It's St. Patrick's day, and Depeche Mode's new album came out.

I was alone in the house. The snow was still sticking on the ground. So why not? I drove to the vinyl record stop to pick up the new album.

I found the LP to the left of "new releases." The friendly old manager was still there.

"Ahh! You came to pick up the new Depehce Mode album! Yeah, that's the last one left!"

I was excited they had it on vinyl. I didn't feel like looking for any other record. I wanted to get out of the store quickly and go back home to listen to it.

Two years ago, I remember picking up Yukihiro Takahashi's *Neuromantic* album from that same guy.

As I head back home, my GPS took me on a route that was very nostalgic and familiar. Namely, there was a certain location I use to go all the time. Her name was viable on the map.

…But when I got home, I just wanted to listen to the album and forget about that.

Dave, Martin and Andy, standing in the snow. Strange because it looked exactly like the snow outside.

My mom came in the kitchen about the same time when the record was playing, "The Worse Crime." She had to go back and visit grandma's house. I helped her get in some groceries as the record played.

Mom got me sushi like always. The California roll from Wegmans that always fell apart. Not truly authentic.

I was eating the flimsy sushi while listening to "You Move." A good song. I liked the bass.

I was happy to hear that the first Gore song was "Eternal." However, it was way too short. Not good enough.

In fact, half the songs on the album were recorded in 2015, and the other half 2016.

In 2015, I was suffering in that... girl's school.

March, that same year (two years ago actually), she admitted cheating on me.

...And as I passed by her house, the place I use to go all the time, I felt her.

Spirit sounds incredibly flat. The same style that KMFDM is producing now. I felt like they were rehashing old lyrics and images over and over again and trying to create original material with it.

I think the producers are thinking way too much about how *they* think about Depeche Mode as a brand. I feel "Where's The Revolution?" is a mimic of "People are People," along with some Beatles worship.

Now, I have a bad memory of when they played in New York City in September of 2013. I was in my dorm room in Philadelphia. That girl casually took the train to see me often. And on the way back, after we kissed, she told me she met with a friend on the way back.

I could not trust her.

I was doing homework that week. I said to myself, "What if I had tickets, got on the bus to New York, and saw Depeche Mode live. That would be so exciting!"

That never happened. I was too afraid to go by myself. I still am afraid to go alone.

I remember trying to catch a Taxi to go play Netrunner at Drexel. That didn't happen either. It was the first week of college and I had homework to do. I was way too cowardly.

And I remember giving that girl an expensive $60 present on Christmas. I did the same on her birthday. *Shadow over Camelot* and *Ticket To Ride*. I would also send her handmade letters too.

I was in love with her.

And every single time she would stalk me and play board games with me and my friends, I fell for it.

She was old trauma. I forgot about her when I found a new girl (I think). …Yet again, she came back.

The best track on Spirit is "Fail." I don't know why Martin Gore keeps a low profile. It has always been a tradition that Gore contributes two songs on every Depeche Mode album. Those tracks on Spirit were "Eternal" and "Fail." Fail is the best track on the entire album.

The lyrics go something like this:

People, do we call this trying?
We're hopeless, forget the denying
Our souls are corrupt
Our minds are messed up
Our consciences, bankrupt
Oh, we're fucked

People, what are we thinking?
It's shameful, our standards are sinking
We're barely hanging on
Our spirit has gone
And once where it shone
I hear a lonesome song

People, how are we coping?
It's futile to even to even start hoping
That justice will prevail
That truth will tip the scales
Our dignity has sailed
Oh, we've failed

…People have lost their sanity, not because they are bad people, but because we have lost this game called "life."

How can you lose in this game called life? It's not like there are any specific rules to it. One has to be living and breathing to enjoy life, right? But once you're dead, that's it! We could say that life is but a dream, or a ticking clock towards death. Once the clock strikes 12, you're done.

Now that's a very hedonist and nihilistic way of thinking. Since this is what every white American likes to think about. Unlike the natural way of following your "dasein," as Martin Heidegger wrote in *Being and Time*, where we prepare ourselves for death and self-improve our existence for future generation.

If we were free to do what we want, however, people would play a Machiavellian game of social networking, dependency, and selfishness.

The human "spirit,' what Gore calls it, is innate within us all. We have the 'spirit' to go forth and to do good in the world. We have a religious "spirit." But what happens if this spirit becomes corrupted? Does it leave the body? Or does the spirit become corrupted?

If the spirit is corrupted, then we worship totalitarian politics. I'm talking about the Alt-Right, Cultural Marxism, the cult of any personality. The "militancy" we feel as a sense of belonging to something greater. ...And then they go ahead and exploit those who go against this rule.

The front cover of Spirit ironically features marching feet and flags flying. A sense of marching nationalism. The 'spirit' of an ideology.

With songs like "Going Backwards," "Where's the Revolution," "The Worst Crime," all bring out some kind of totalitarian politics.

But "Fail" brings out the album's theme. People have failed the social game. It's time to consider that things are bad because they are innately bad, that people have failed to win a game they could never win in the first place. Like how I failed to woo over that girl. And she failed to understand me. Or that she failed with her own poor choices.

We failed trying to make friends in high school, we failed trying to chase after our dreams, we failed trying to live with certain people we wanted to live with, we failed getting the job, we failed and don't have a narrative or legacy to tell other people about.

Even if you had those things, and for once you were the winner, people are still failing.

F. Roger Devlin's book, *Sexual Utopia in Power*, is about how men fail to achieve the women they desire. The women also fail to understand the men. Both parties have failed.

Gore's lyrics again:

People, how are we coping?
It's futile to even to even start hoping
That justice will prevail
That truth will tip the scales
Our dignity has sailed
Oh, we've failed

Erik Erikson had something called "the stages of pyschosocial development." This was a psychological theory that describe peoples trying to answer basic questions about their own existence. The right questions

42

answered would mean to live a "good life." But if one fails to answer these spiritual questions, they become corrupted.

The Hollywood Neo-nazi is living in his own traumas. In other words, he failed the psychosocial game. Meanwhile, the jolly cultural marxist professor had the wrong answers. Both are ironically perverted.

People fail in the psychosocial paradigm. They fail answering questions and will fail with perverted answers.

The reason why everyone is miserable in the western world is because everyone has failed individually as a player in a game that they don't know how to play. Basically, there are winners, and there are losers.

...And losers listen to Depeche Mode.

I have to ask myself whether I failed in the social game, or whether I am an exploited pawn with no influence, just like the protagonist in Albert Camus's *The Stranger.* Was I offered the good life? And in order to win it, did I have to pretend to be like Roosh V or be ripped like Jack Donovan? Did I lose because I failed to seize these crucial life moments? Is it because of social Darwinism?

And that girl, who I knew since the 4th grade. I still drive by her house as I pass the record store. I told her all my

43

secrets, and tried so hard to win her as my girlfriend, and hopefully future wife.

But it didn't happen. Either I lost and made the wrong choices, or she failed and didn't see me. Maybe I lost because I had to answer those psychosocial questions while she was still in high school.

Am I a non-influential agent, or loser in this game?

I feel like my own spirit has been transformed into something else. Call it, "overcoming my youthful trauma." But I think it's more than that. Then again, the spirit of me is energized into something else (the creation of art).

She lost her spirit to acknowledge me. I lost my spirit when it didn't get through with her.

I failed to woo her. Now I'm an Asian-Aryan.

3-18-17

Weeb Nationalism

LARPing has become a recent phenomenon with white Americans.

The upper-middle class is chasing after (and naively believing) the elite aristocratic dream. The truth is that the upper class is nothing but decadent. The youthful upper class is into hardcore punk, the avant-garde arts, and have all flirted with the Antifa (not to mention, gotten at least some Asian pussy). Ironically, the upper-class is excessively educated and stuck at a corporate or academic job. It would make sense that the class below them clean up their shit after the party.

That leaves us with the LARPing nature of the middle and lower classes.

What I mean by "Live-Action-Role-Playing," is not Larry Niven's *Dream Park* version of it, but our people acting out social roles that don't accord with reality. All LARPers are soft escapist.

A "weeb" (or wapanese) is a term for a young white person that believes he is "Japanese" or a living "anime" character. I put "Japanese" and "anime" in quotation marks because this is not the true definition of the terms, but a superficial one crafted by white people.

The word "Japananimation" predated "anime" in the western market. But "anime" is casually used to sound authentic to its original meaning. Unfortunately, the word "Japananimation" meant cyberpunk, sci-fi, and bloody pulp cartoons. The word "anime" has been placed by this definition (maybe at this time period, it has something to do with high school girls).

This is the discipline of orientalism. The most famous critic of orientalism was Edward Said. Although he was arguing against Judeo-Christian culture taking control of Palestine (Said has some sort of crypto-anti-semitism within him, excluding some anti-white remarks he would have made).

If we were to understand orientalism by definition, then we could never have an absolute truth of the other side. Foreigners are speculating what exactly is "The Other."

When Americans tried to make "animes" of their own, we got *Avatar: The Last Airbender, RWBY*, and *Teen Titans*. We have a "simulacra" of anime and not the authentic thing (as written by Jean Baudrillard).

All LARPers are simulacrums of what they desire to be and how they want the world to perceive them.

My Japanese neighbors once told me about the nature of white people. "They are like bulls in a china shop. They have pointy noses, hunch all the time, and leave a mess where ever they go. Watch them eat Japanese food and look how hard they try to emulate us!" The Japanese will only criticize white people when no one is looking.

If you are at community college, observe a Japanese 101 classroom. Usually it's one of the most popular classes on campus. The class is full of dyed-hair, cosplay LARPers of all kinds. All trying to learn basic hiragana.

Now compare that to the Chinese 101 class, you get dedicated students trying to learn the language.

Odd isn't it? Why is Japanese 101 so popular then? It's from the popularity of anime!

This has made the Alt-Right criticize anime, calling it "Chinese Cartoons" and "degenerate." The logic is that it is not made by white people, therefore, it is globalist consumerism to keep the white working class sedated.

The manosphere "Gamers" would argue to go physically outside and get laid. (How many times have you heard that?)

It seems there is no room on the Alt-Right to like anime, as it is "unnatural" for whites to consume it. Only the "premium anime" (Jorjani again) can be observed and cherished by western culture, like the works of Yukio Mishima.

However, there is no denying the aesthetic and cultural influence of anime upon the whole Gen-X and Millennial generations of white Americans. The medium cannot be thrown away so fast.

What are we to do with all these LARPers and anime aficionados?

…Convert them to Weeb Nationalism.

Politics online is extremely petty, like micro genres of sub genres of music. Anything we can consume can be considered a "lifestyle" choice. Even "white nationalism" can be a business for Red Ice Radio, making all the promises in the world that they are starting "the revolution," when in reality, it's a living for Henry and Lana.

America has an interesting philosophy. "Do whatever you can to exploit the weak and make your dream a reality." This American philosophy should not get in the way of any serious political movement. (Have you ever noticed that you only have to be a consumer reading alt-right websites to be on a phishing report?) LARPers are all consumers.

But nationalism, or any political ideology, will give them more freedom (maybe).

Nationalism for weebs means an exclusive collective of like-minded weebs together.

...Exactly like a Discord server.

The ethnostate ideology is getting the internet forum world and making into an IRL reality. Everyone's little perversion, whether that may be Gay Furry Communism, Asexual Goth Board Gamers, Tranny Sci-Fi Readers, or The African-American Dead Simpsons society, ethnostates will make their private clubs a working reality!

This is why nationalism will become more important in the coming decades. Technology will improve people's liberty.

However, weebs can be anything from the clubs I just stated. Some weebs will think nationalism is "racist."

Realize, there are hardly any black, hispanic, or non-white/ Asian weebs out there. If there was one, he would be that token nonwhite person for preening purposes.

The truth is that all weebs are white people.

If weebs would realize this, they would gather collectively towards white nationalism. But it is not that easy for them to do…

There is a large faction of weebs that like to believe they are something else, other than white. Sounds ironic, yes?

Most weebs I have encounter are white people that wish they were Japanese or that "anime" was real.

It is not uncommon for a white weeb to find himself an Asian lover.

I have written about this phenomenon and have called it "Asian-Aryanism." Asian-Aryanism would sound like a contradiction to white nationalism, as it is biracial nationalism for whites and Asians. However, it is still "based" (as-much-as-I-fucking-hate-that-word) nationalism.

Weebs have three choices with their lifestyle:

1. LARP as something they are not (An asian or an anime character) and accidentally create Asian-Aryanism (Eurasian kids).

2. LARP as something they are not, find another white weeb, and propagate white genes (cultural placebo).

3. Realize they are white, and will continue to take pride in their interest in anime, and join The Anime Right (LARPy Neo-Nazism, materialist white nationalism).

4. (*Did you see this one coming?*) Dump weeb culture altogether and call it a "phase" in their life.

Ironically though, most white weebs will fail to find an Asian lover, and will end up naturally with a white significant other. This white lover, however, may also be a weeb. Both cannot be aware of their whiteness, and then ironically raise a white weeb family together. This is exactly what I call by an authentic definition, "weeb nationalism." It's not about knowing or being aware of what you're doing, but existence becomes so natural that they don't question it.

I feel that The Anime Right wishes to "awaken" these naive weebs that marry their own white kin. Or at least show them *Counter-Currents*, *Radix Journal*, *American Renaissance*, or *The Daily Stormer* (bad taste). There can be weebs who take pride in racial nationalism and still be some kind of LARPer.

Unfortunately, it's still LARPing.

51

The most effective strategy would be number 2. That is, Let white weebs breed and make them *believe* they are something they are not! All they want to do, as natural Stuff-White-People-Like citizens, is irrationally be a white person under universal consumerism (as much as I fucking hate every normie who does this).

Ha, well, this is why The Anime Right is significant. Eventually, you have to point the Elephant in the room, that is, white people acting like white people. Even if they all get mad at you.

Remember, they have three choices, "Weeb Nationalism," "The Anime Right," or "Asian-Aryanism."

…Too hard to think about? I think we can all agree that the new episodes of *Samurai Jack* are really good! But if you want my true opinion… Fuck The Anime Right! Asian-Aryanism forever!

3-22-17

"White," "Asian," or "Eurasian?"

The biggest obstacle unifying the Eurasian identity is the struggle of the racial labels "white," or "asian."

Jennifer Suzuki wrote in *Confessions of a Submissive East Asian Woman,* that being "white" is the safest way to go. I disagree.

It's a simple answer. White people need to be "yellow-pilled" into Asian-Aryanism. Whitewashed Asians would naturally come to the collective when white guys show their pride in Asian-Aryanism.

But the normie doesn't understand why the word "Asian-Aryan" should be fought over. Why choose the word "Aryan," when this has nothing to do with the Middle-East tribes of Iran?

Obviously, "Aryan" is used in the whimsical sense. In fact, the correct term should be "Eurasian." It's a joke that a "master race" will be eventually fulfilled. Thus, "Asian-Aryanism," is a coming master race that mixes both the great achievements of whites and asian civilization. This does not mean white or Asian genocide. This is a natural phenomenon that Eurasian millennials will become a part of. Hegemonic white and asian people will be conserved in the process.

"Asian-Aryan," is a playful internet meme. It sounds like a skinhead with an Asian girlfriend, or a nerdy avant-garde college kid and his artsy-fartsy Asian girlfriend. "Asian-Arynaism" as a word has its roots with the punk rock subculture. Already, we have such cultural things as "Health Goths," "Seapunk," and "Furries." "Asian-Aryanism" is one of many new influential subcultures. (I can thank *Amped Asia* for getting the Asian-Aryan subculture out there).

But being more serious, Asian-Aryanism will find a future cause. A new name shall appear like "Pan-Eurasinism," "Eurasianism," or "Asiansexuality." They will become the surrogate names found on a future Wikipedia page. Asian-Aryanism is an umbrella term, conglomerating all influenced subcultures on the internet. This is the same way the "Alt-Right" accepted all right-wing and reactionary ideologies. Asian-Aryanism will do the same with Asian culture and thought in the western perspective.

However, the Asian-Aryan identity struggles in our culture is because there is no words or clubs defending the unknown interest. The first word to appear a decade ago was "wapanese," a derogatory term for a white kid that believes he is a living anime character. Since then, the word has evolved into "weeb" and still enjoys a presence in internet culture.

Also in the past year, "The Anime Right," has been formed and represents a National Socialist interest in Eastern culture. Still, they associate with extreme white nationalist politics. We see movements that flirt with Asian-Aryanism, but don't go towards the next step.

This is the problem with unifying people under the same interest. Asian-Aryanism is stuck between the position of being considered a white man's movement or an Asian infiltration project.

So, which one of these is it? The answer is neither.

Asian-Aryanism is a third-position party looking for its own identity beyond white or Asian culture. At the same time, Asian-Aryanism respects both the white and Asian races. Asian-Aryanism belongs to the sons and daughters of two beautiful civilizations.

Asian-Aryanism is against cuck-minded politics, two-sided answers, anti-white rhetoric, and arrogant white/Asian supremacists.

Asian-Aryanism will respect white nationalism and appreciate the culture of Western Civilization, while distancing itself and finding its own Eurasian culture for greater meaning. Arrogant cultures of Asia will try and get all the Eurasians on their side for their battle, but Asian-Aryans should look out for their own interests first, and not of the foreign interest of their parents. We may take wisdom from them, but it's up to us to have a future for our children.

If a Eurasian decides to be associated as "white" or "asian," he or she is looking for an ultimate amnesty, and rather feels comfortable being around one of the two people. Unfortunately, the hegemonic races of "white" and "asian" will do their best to cover up the Eurasian identity as nonexistent. Eurasians have two possible answers, but have no future destiny.

I understand many of my Eurasian friends choose "white" or "asian" because they want to feel safe in a normative society. I respect both sides as well. But the point of Asian-Aryanism is to reach the third position. A new position that respects both sides while it struggles to find a new unity and identity.

I would like the following five groups co-existing with one another. They also have to be friendly and supportive towards each other, like family members:

1. White-male/Asian-female and Asian-male/White-female couples.

2. White-Weebs and Whitewashed-Asians.

3. Half/Hafu/Hapa/Eurasian people.

4. People with "central" Asian blood (Kazakhstan for example).

5. Any disenfranchised whites or Asians that want to join in and commit to the Eurasian identity (like the concept of American immigration).

Asian-Aryanism is against the Kalergi plan. We have no foundations with Judeo-Christian culture. Rather, the two cultures of Christianity and Asian religions will be mixed together, creating a bastard one. ...Go to church on Sunday, Shinto prayers at home.

Asian-Aryanism is a bond between two parties, whites and Asians. Other non-races, like blacks and Mexicans, might show interest in Eurasian culture. But Asian-Aryanism looks out for its own interest, and slams the door upon these darker races. If blacks and Mexicans like Asian culture, let them start their own bicultural institutions. We believe human bio-diversity *and* biculturalism is true cultural diversity. It's for the greater good and health towards world civilization.

Asian-Aryanims has no ill feelings towards non-Eurasian people. Race, IQ, genetics, and evolution is a true part of life. If race mixing were to occur with Eurasians, then the Kalergi plan would come into effect. Asian-Aryanism is against multiculturalism and the egalitarian philosophy of the globalized world. Multiculturalism should be practice in its own country, not the world.

Asian-Aryanism sounds confusing to the alt-right because we promote race-mixing. Again, Asian-Aryanism is against universal race mixing. There is already a large Asian-American culture that was birthed by a previous generation of race-mixers. Asian-Aryanism is a cultural movement for these lost people.

Asian-Aryanism is an umbrella term to describe the cultural movement between whites and Asians. It is an avant-garde institution that is saving a generation of children from the claws of the multicultural and globalist paradigm. Asian-Aryanism goes beyond the petty conflict of racially arrogant whites and bug-like Asians that thrive towards world domination.

We are Eurasian striving towards higher levels of culture and civilization.

3-28-17

Aesthetically Pleasing Men in *King of Fighters XIV*

Amped Asia published an article titled, *"Top 10 Asian Femme Fatales in Fighting Games."*[2]

Any young white boy growing up in the Midwest and addicted to video games would fall for any of these oriental beauties, and this would encourage the concept of Asian-Aryanism.

I felt the same nostalgia myself when it came to Nakoruru from *Samurai Shodown* and Mai from *The King of Fighters* that are also featured in the countdown.

I am a huge SNK fanboy. I am quite mad that Chun-li took the #1 spot. *"No offense to Chinese girls. You're the best!"*

Growing up, I had a Neo-Geo and would play games like *NAM-1975, Magician Lord, Metal Slug X, Waku Waku 7*, and most importantly, *The King of Fighters '98*.

---

2 http://www.ampedasia.com/article/top-10-asian-femme-fatales-fighting-games/

SNK recently released *The King of Fighters XIV* and dropped the sister name "Playmore" to go back to their classical roots. I am quite thrilled by this decision.

The SNK cult has been around since the 80's and has survived that last few decades. SNK ruled the cyberpunk video arcade market of Japan (influencing the work of William Gibson) and slowly lost that power to Square Enix and Capcom. Capcom now selfishly claims themselves as the new ruler of "competitive arcade games."

The brand *Street Fighter* is a household name. The game depicts racial stereotypes and a nostalgia feast for American players, like what *Star Wars: The Force Awakens* did for Star Wars fans. I never did get into Street Fighter. *Street Fighter 3: Third Strike* was the pinnacle of the series. I was quite good at the game in my college years. However, the passionate community behind *King of Fighters 2002* and *Garou: Mark of the Wolves* was too tempting, and so I refused to play Capcom games since then.

SNK was "Japanese arcade culture" before there even was one. They were the first company to shift the anime dramas, like yaoi and shojo, into their games. Characters like Iori Yagami made KOF feel more alive than a simple color palette change of Ryo to Ken. Iori was cool. Any fat stay-at-home Asian girl would fall for him. KOF felt like a moving anime, not just a generic fighting game. Take a look at what was accomplished in KOF 12 and 13.

Now entering the realm of 3D, SNK has many challenges ahead of them.

Some have criticized The King of Fighters as being that "gay yaoi anime fighter" or "that knock-off of Street Fighter," which are misconceived claims.

First, KOF has a better and easier fighting system than SF. Most people who get into the game never leave the addiction. SF is a popularity contest and relies more on consuming than the competition itself. ("Gamer" is a disgusting term I don't like being associated with. All it means is "consumer").

And second, yes, KOF has a cast of handsome and sexy men any Asian boy would look up to.

That's quite a contradictory statement, since Amped Asia wrote the article for a straight and heterosexual audience.

Asian-Aryanism needs to have powerful and aesthetically-pleasing men. That is, strong men that are role models for a future society and race.

White and Asian men are often told that they cannot appreciate the beauty of men, otherwise they are "gay" or potential pedophiles.

Elliot Rodger went on his massacre because he could not get a girlfriend. He could have ventilated his anger through KOF and roleplayed as Rock Howard. Rodger would have joined the masses of Asian-Americans that strive to be greater by playing KOF.

A lot of Asian kids I know play KOF and look up to the fictional men. My one Chinese friend has told me over and over again that he wants to be like Shen Woo. They have the same personalities. Another friend I know, nicknamed "Asian Andy," told me that he wanted to be Kim Kaphwan at the age of 8.

I love KOF because of the fighters. I first learned about the anime *Akira* through the KOF character K9999, a blatant rip-off of Tetsuo (and dons the same voice actor, Nozomu Sasaki). My KOF 2002 teams has always been Ryuji Yamazaki, Angel, and Seth. I love the angry "street-culture" they portray. Not only that, but they all have a unique self-defensive play style.

SF does not offer this cool identity KOF has. KOF is full of aesthetically pleasing men as well as beautiful Asian women.

I will give some examples of great men in the KOF 14,

–Benimaru Nikaido is a Eurasian super model and lady killer. His broken English and sexy clothes woo over everyone.

–Shun'Ei is a sexy Chinese yaoi teenager that wears a tie and belongs in a K-pop band.

-Along with his best (and not-so-gay) friend, Meitenkun, a young boy that wants to sleep all the time and cuddle. This gives the impression that he wants to cuddle with all of his girl fans (he is a living *dakimakura*).

–Kukri is emo. He represents all mentally disturbed and angry Asian kids that failed to shoot up the school. Now they all master his combo move set.

–Ramon is a pretty cool womanizer that kicks people across the other side of the screen.

–K' is a chaotic neutral badass. He is neither good or bad and does his own thing. Every single girl wants to sleep with him and every single guy wishes they were a lone wolf like him.

–Hein is a butler with a sadomasochistic background. Clean cut, handsome, good paying job… but once you're with him, he's got some very strange perversions in bed.

–Rock Howard is a fan favorite. How many times did anyone wish they were like him?

I can go on with the many male fighters in KOF. Other games, like *Tekken* and *Virtua Fighter,* also have a male dominated cast featuring many guys to look up to.

Reading this, you might think I am gay or promoting homosexuality in Asian-Aryanism. I am ok with pro-gay Asian-Aryan politics, so as long as they don't hurt the greater good and are in favor of promoting and propagating Eurasian genes and aesthetics.

I loved both yaoi and shojo at a young age. When I first discovered yaoi, I couldn't believe that there were extremely handsome and kind men. I always have tried to emulate the behavior of a yaoi character in real life.

There are a majority of weebs that try and pretend to be other male characters from the latest boy-related anime shows. Often these shows are from the "boys" perspective and less about how the "girls" see things. Asian-Aryanism is on the path of creating Eurasian children that will look radically beautiful and similar to the characters we watch in animes.

The Greeks admired the body and strength of Adonis. A man like Hercules was a true hero. In our lonely and deprived society, we all look up to the aesthetically pleasing men in KOF. Good fictional men will lead us towards greatness of character and spirt. Any girl would dream of being the wife of a real-life Rock Howard. Asian-Aryan genes will propagate to eventually create Rock Howard-looking children. Only by a healthy society and civilization with men and women that uphold it.

Amped Asia is doing their part by showing men that Asian women are worth obtaining. SNK gives the disenfranchised Asian-American community and weebs the power to role play and fulfill the aggressive energy of guys they want to be like.

I'm grateful I grew up playing KOF. It's a game and universe where weebs/Asian/Eurasian males can be better men.

3-31-17

Erik Erikson's Pyschosocialism: An Introduction

Erik Erikson is a psychologist best known for his theory of "psychosocial development." It is a psychoanalytical theory that identifies birth and death through eight "stages." Each stage is a challenge that the person confronts. Life presents obstacles, and the person questions his reality.

"Am I gay?"

"Do I like sports?"

"Am I an artist?"

"Do I like Asian women?"

As you can see, many things can unfold in one's environmental and cultural upbringing. Why is Erikson's theory of "pyschosocialism" so relevant towards the truth?

In the internet troll subculture, we have mastered analyzing the life of the boring "normie" and tend to make fun of their nature. The normie goes through the psychosocial narrative asking the same questions we do. But what if we have the wrong answers to our life questions? Do we live a "bad" life? What are the "good" answers?

Those who have odd answers are called "LARPers." This is not about *Dagorhir Battle Games*. This is about people who role play realities not according to their own. Every single weeb is likely roleplaying an anime character they like. The young white kid associates life with watching anime and has learned morals from the shows he ~~was watching~~ watches. The psychosocial narrative told him, "what are you doing in your teenage years?" The boy responses back by watching anime. In his early twenties (the next stage), the psychosocial narrative will ask again, "who are you, what do you do, and who is your girlfriend?" The boy will forcefully struggle to find answers, dying his hair blue, hanging out at the board game store, and having a (possibly Asian) girlfriend that thinks she too is an anime character. Everyone is answering questions from a pyschosocial narrative that is forced upon us.

Another psychologist I must mention is Albert Bandura. Bandura is known for his "Bobo doll experiment." The argument presented in his experiment is that children are born blank slates and learn everything from role models. Of course, this sounds totally left-wing and bogus. However, if taken into consideration, Erik Erikson's philosophy is a companion piece to Bandura's social learning theory.

If Bandura argues that every human being imitates another (monkey see, monkey do), then Erikson's philosophy argues for *the creation of the self* which others will imitate. Bandura and Erikson are an endless Ying-Yang cycle.

"Which came first? The chicken, or the egg?"

Are we really the atomized individuals we in the west like to see ourselves? Or are we merely imitating everyone else and trying to answer life's questions that come crashing down on use like an avalanche?

If we are talking about "The Alt-Right," "Furries," "Gamers," "Goths," "Hardcore punks," whatever... One word should put an end to all of this: Psychosocialism.

We are all LARPers, face it.

You are not living out a special life that is unique to your existence. You are picking up a VHS Tape of someone else's previous life and roleplaying it out. You may try so hard to be different than everyone else. In the end, you are looking for nothing.

The college professors, the police officers, the intellects, the athletes... they all have psychosocial narratives.

To disturb one's narrative and existence creates problems. Try disturbing the feminist psychosocial narrative and see what she has to say to you.

"You must be a sexist and a racist!"

Heard this before? When people call names, they are mad you are doubting their reality. If life is utterly meaningless, most will go on a "fatalist" or nihilist way of thinking. Some even commit suicide. To doubt one's life requires a complete re-examination of everything they have been answering since they were a toddler. It is death if you try to answer this at the age of 25.

Teen romances and animes portray the young and naive protagonist getting the girl and living life "happily ever after," once he overcomes the obstacles presented to him.

In psychosocialism, you're either a "winner" or a "loser."

I could go on about the "light" and "dark" side of the questions of "winning and losing," but I don't mean to recite everything I know about psychosocialism.

I would like to address the question towards Asian-Aryanism.

Most people are depressed because they feel they are "losers" to other psychosocial narratives. Weak people will also mock and imitate other people's lives to feel good about themselves (Bandura). Human beings simply cannot be aware of the psychosocial narrative all the time. But it helps to understand the meaning behind why "normies" and odd subcultures act the way they do.

Martin Heidegger tried to create peace within pyschosocialism. (He came before Erikson, and Erikson based his theories around Heidegger). Heidegger argued that being loyal to your "dasein" ~~was~~ is a good thing. That understanding what is "authentic" and "inauthentic" is a struggle in life.

Suppose you live your life as an Amish person on a farm. However, when your parents are not looking, you hang out at the local community college and pretend you are an anime character. This is psychosocialism in action. This is where you ask the question, "do I like anime?" and the answer follows, "other kids like anime, therefore, I should like anime too."

Now, let's say that your biological nature comes from Amish genes, and you have a natural upbringing around the farm. You hate it, but you can compromise with it. According to Heidegger, being loyal to your dasein would mean getting rid of your inauthentic anime subculture and associating yourself more with farming. This is the original destiny life has given to you.

Oddly enough, Heidegger was a Nazi. What does that tell you?

If we were all loyal to our daseins and "authentic" towards life, we wouldn't have to worry about the pyschosocial narrative. Everything that Erikson said would be just a theory. Whenever we may ask these big questions to ourselves, we are only trying to naturally find the pursuit of wisdom and happiness.

Normies don't question the authority of life. They have simple answers. You the reader, and I, are doubting existence.

We both came across those big questions in life, where we had to ask about our sexuality, our health, the friends we chose, and our careers. Liberals tell us we can do anything in our life! But they happen to go through *the best* pyschosocial narratives.

Healthy people can dismantle the naivety of the LARPing, pyschosocial narrative. Social Justice Warriors, The Antifa, Feminists… they are LARPing identities because their lives need meaning. Each group is trapped in a bubble. "You're the bad guy, I'm the good guy, this is my lover, I belong here, and I don't care who you are unless you're benefiting my life."

This sounds like everyone is a protagonist to an anime no one is watching. But they are watching their own show.

We as Asian-Aryans are aware of our existence. Many of these ignorant "nu-cucks" live life like an anime, and have no true loyalty towards their dasein.

71

We were once weebs, Asian-studies students, Asiansexuals, whitewashers, civic nationalist, gamers, punk rockers, leftist, artist, and everyday normies that tried to climb the supposed social ladder to get what we wanted. We answered questions that tried to make sense of our true realities.

Asian-Aryanism is an honest answer to the psychosocial problem. No longer do we have to suffer from the "hubris" of life. All the anxiety of trying to live out a psychosocial narrative goes away. We become beings that are honest to what we want in life. We may still LARP to feel good about ourselves. But in the end, we took the yellow-pill.

LARPing is a disease among the west. I felt that Heidegger was only trying to synthesize Eastern philosophy into the West. We have lost that tradition. What has been created, is the selfish "existential" postmodern ego that is psychosocialism.

Either we play the psychosocial game, or we break out of it by being loyal to Heidegger's dasein.

Asian-Aryanism is a protest against pyschosocialism and the lame existence of mundane life. We strive towards excellence for an honest and open Asian-Aryan subculture and a future society.

Pyschosocialism is a lesson about our decadent society. Let's have good answers and not LARP for them.

4-1-17

A Letter for Tyrone

Alright Tyrone, pull up your pants and stop watching *Afro Samurai*, because this is serious.

I know how much you look up to Billy Blanks and Jero, but this isn't about them. This about you.

I care about every person on this planet. I wish that everyone would follow their own destiny and start to associate with people like themselves. That would mean that ethnonationalism is a good for all peoples on the planet. Multiculturalism and diversity have failed humanity greatly.

…Hold up Tyrone, I know what you're thinking.

"Without dese white people, us black people wouldn't have no place to survive. Without them, we screwed!"

Or you might be thinking about that other thought,

"Damn dat white devil! He be oppressin' every person on dis planet! Black Lives Matter should be about black people first! And whitey is going to pay for everything!"

This thought soon follows with the classic, "Plato stole it from us. You see, we wuz kangs!"

And Tyrone, your answer is "gibsmedat."

I don't know whether gibsmedat is a part of African-American culture or blacks worldwide. But hear this Tyrone, I am not going to give you anything.

And now you like "anime" because some of your white friends have been watching it too. You favorite so-called "anime" is *The Boondocks*.

I get it, you want to watch media that shows you were kangz. But let's not talk about W.E.B. Du Bois or Booker T. Washington, and rather let us focus on Asian culture.

…Tyrone, have you ever sank yourself into some asian puss-say? No. You haven't. …Maybe into some Jungle Asians, I don't know.

Do I care if your one-quarter Japanese? Does that give you the right to listen to rap and live off welfare?

Here we are back to the concept of "gibsmedat." If whitey is successful, you want to take it down. You want what he wants. If whitey got himself some nice Asian poontang, you want it too.

But listen mah nigga, "Asian-Aryanism" is not for you.

I personally love the quirky personality and loyal behavior of black girls. Accordingly, White Male / Black Females have the lowest divorce rate and biggest families (Pew Research). ...Take note, there are black girls that want hugggeee monster white cock.

Now, is there a collective of White Male / Black Females? What about the dreaded Black Male / White Female? They unfortunately have the highest divorce rate and largest number of illegitimate children!

It turns out our WMBF are agents for the "Oreo" or mulatto race. However, once your black, you never go back. To counter against this, white dads try and make sure their half black kids think and be like whitey. Sorry, but it's better than taking *The Holy Tablets* seriously.

White men and women hardly get the control in their black interracial marriage. The children automatically become "black" and their "white" part is shunned. What a pity.

Tyrone, think about your offspring with that Vietnamese thot you scored with. Will your son be "black?" Or will he

76

realize that "black" culture is horrible and would rather associate with the Asian side instead?

This is called "black privilege." The feeling when your mixed children realize that half their blood belongs to an unworthy and dishonorable race of primitive monkey people.

For example, (as said by a common blasian), "I am sorry sensei, I have black privilege. This blood will not influence my way of thinking!"

Why would you want every single half-black Asian to act like a nigger?

Tyrone, I know you don't want that. You may say, "dat be rasis!," but I care about you.

I believe in the Chinese-Jamaican people. They are a beautiful people with their own culture and institution. Charming and peaceful. It is quite possible for an Afro-Asian collective to happen with them.

But please Tyrone, understand you are not white.

Other blacks I know hate the race-mixing paradigm going on right now. They hate that Time/National Geographic magazine of *"This is what people will look like in the year 3000."* A majority of African-Americans don't want to have gook and cracker genes within them. They want to be... black people!

And I know some other passive-aggressive and low IQ black people get soooo gibsmedat when they want The Kalergi Plan to come in effect.

"Bratha, we can truly be grateful, if we mix wit every race on dis planet! Everyone will become a nigga and weez can make da pyramids again!"

I hope you don't think like that Tyrone. That is a poor understanding of race, IQ, and intelligence.

Face it, multiculturalism and diversity was a lie. It didn't make you better. The Jewish elites took your money, and the quiet white guy took the Asian girl. You were left alone in poverty, while the media portrays you in every single commercial and movie as the good guy to worship. Whites bow down and make your life special. We white people want to commit suicide so we can make nonwhites the white people of the future.

I know that isn't you Tyrone. I know you thought about The Jewish Question too.

And Tyrone, you think it's okay to be an expert on Asian culture?

I have to applaud you if you go in this direction. First, you eventually lose that nigger culture of yours when you assimilate. Second, your mind will drain, refilling it with Asian thought. And finally, you will grow "black privilege," realizing you were never worthy of anything in Asian culture.

If you ever get to that point, I think it is best to create your own Afro-Asian institution.

But Tyrone, as an Asian-Aryan myself, please I am not going to help you with your problems. Not even if your handicapped or know you are innately retarded. Stop playing gibsmedat on me. I have nothing to give you.

I care about you Tyrone, I really do. Asian-Aryanism is a bond between white and Asian people only. The black races can't fit into the shoes of western and eastern cultures. … But you have your pyramids, don't you?

If you really wanted an Asian maiden to help you on your esoteric pyramid quest, then dump your gibsmedat culture and create a new mythology. The blood of Asians would increase your IQ and will give you peace within the world.

79

But please, please-please-please Tyrone, you are not going to get any Asian-Aryan blood from us. There is a place called "Brazil" and it's perfect for you.

I don't know if you will ever start an Afro-Asian institution, but I am not going to help you create. No. Never. Not even to preen or to show "I'm a good person."

We can still be friends Tyrone, but please, do your own thing.

…But let me tell you mah brudda. I love Jungle Asians, Ganguro Culture, Asian hip-hop, Ariana Miyamoto, and Afro-Asian girls in general. You can take pride in that.

And for Christ sake, Adrian Tomine went out of his way to put you on the front cover of *The New Yorker*![3]

Are you happy now? Or do still need some more gibsmedat?

Tyrone, reality is harsh. Let's respect each other's space and shake hands. Please don't disturb my people, and I won't disturb yours.

---

3 https://www.newyorker.com/magazine/2017/01/02

Asian-Aryanism isn't for you. It's for whites and Asians. You can be a race realist and be an ally for the cause, I would love that. And in return, I will advocate Afro-Asian culture.

As whites and Asians, we have our own racial and interracial problems to deal with. We don't need yours.

Maybe you're with R.A. The Rugged Man, who believes those evil "whites and Asians" are up to no good, or maybe you will you respect our destiny? We certainly will respect yours if you do.

And one final note Tyrone, I don't have anything for you. There is no special meme magic for black people getting those rare Asian girls. White guys get Asian girls instantly. That's just a fact.

Please, do your own thing Tyrone. Transhumanism is the enemy.

4-3-17

The Other White Girl

The reason why white men are at a fast rate are choosing Asian women is because their female companions have failed them. White women have shifted towards narcissism, snobbery, and feminism, which acts as an ideology for the white bourgeois class.

White women have been trying way too hard to emulate the male character. By acting like an ironic, SWPL-minded beta male, could they possibly attract a mate? White girls fail to understand that this is unattractive.

They don't even understand that biology has something to do with their behavior and thinking patterns. Females were made to take care of the children and provide a "matriarchal" influence over society. Not a "patriarchal" one.

This chaos has interrupted the natural order of things and has lead other white men to create MGTOW, or "Men-Going-Their-Own-Way," to fight against the cruel nature of feminism.

Birth rates are low, divorce is high, and white people have swindled themselves believing they are atomized individuals working around a free market system.

The Alt-Right, "red pill," and civic nationalist movements have been trying to save America from total destruction. However, the outcome is still unpredictable. There might even be a civil war between white people again, and this time divided by the political left and right.

Bourgeois white people run away from physical war. They would rather secretly marry an Asian wife, have three kids, live their life in a boring, mainline, gated-community, and get a huge paycheck every month working for a corporation that exploits the lower classes. This is exactly how the SWPL mind works.

White people, just like any other natural human being on this planet, wants to be left alone. This abstract universal thinking whites cling on to is only complicating things. It becomes a war between People-who-want-to-be-left-alone vs. Those-who-want-you-under-the-influence.

Whites have crafted a rhetoric so advanced, that they could use it to justify their own perversions and freedoms, without any higher authority disturbing them. This philosophy roots itself in the birth of America and the rise of libertarianism (and to one extreme, anarcho-capitalism).

Still, this does not solve the issue between the sexes. This is again upper-class white people running away from their problems and deluding the white middle class with the promise of an authentic and progressive aristocracy. The upper class is decadent and depraved. White people must become "red-pilled" in order to awake from their materialistic slumber.

However, this red-pilling process is not enough to change the minds of every single white person. As an Asian-Aryan, I strongly believe that there is something corrupted about the nature of Western culture and its people. If white people were truly on a "healthy" track of living, they would be happy to associate with any white person. Unfortunately, white people have forced themselves to believe everything is universal and that every human being is a living god.

Today, there is no collective nature within white people. There can be no harmony with Western individualism.

White men at a large rate have given up reproducing white children, and rather seek the benefits of "multiculturalism" and escape through this ideological materialism. Ironically, white men have found foreign love with Asian women and not with any other non-whites. White girls are over-educated and left home alone without a partner. Is it even possible for white men and women to get along?

According to Christian Lander in his book, *Whiter Shades of Pale*, there is a civil war between "The Right Kind of White People," vs. "The Wrong Kind of White People." The Right Kind is trying to eradicate The Wrong Kind, which promotes working-class culture and rude behavior.

84

Ironically, The Right Kind are the promoters of Cultural Marxism and decadent behavior. It is The Wrong Kind that promotes the survival of white people and "healthy" conservative values.

However, from the Asian-Aryan perspective, both sides are bad.

The Wrong Kind will support something like of Jim Goad's *Redneck Manifesto*, which is bad for the health of any natural white person. White people should not adapt the attitudes of The Right Kind or *Apocalypse Culture*. Both The Right and Wrong Kind promote unlivable and painful conditions to any good, meaningful white person.

The only way out of this is through a third position. This is through Asian-Aryanism. But another consideration is pursing "The Other White Girl."

Who is she? And where can you find her?

The Other White Girl is a natural, ignorant, naive, and religious-minded (in the non-spiritual sense) white girl that acts in tune with her inner nature. She is basically an Asian girl with white skin.

For example,

1. They wear normal clothes.

2. They are small in size.

3. They have brown or blonde hair.

4. They have a career which is like being a mother.

5. They love to talk and "relate."

6. They are flat-chested, and possibly a little chubby. A normal plain Jane.

The Alt-Right often argues that this girl can be found in Russia or in a third world European country. That may be true, but in the American context, she is hard to find. Too much of the ugly and decadent culture will proselytize The Other White Girl onto the dark side (and she will become a thot).

This is why white girls can never be trusted from an Asian-Aryan perspective. We love white girls that can submit to the power of Asian culture or find herself an Asian boyfriend. White girls are only redeemable for the Asian-Aryan cause if they become a Weeb Nationalist or one of us.

How many times have your white parents, or even some white friends, told you, as white-on-white wisdom, *"You just have to find the right one!"*

This is another way of saying that you will find The Other White Girl in a sea of already degenerate white people that hate each other.

The Other White Girl is everywhere, but she is losing faith every day. Depression kick in, and she falls into MTV decadent culture at a young age. I suggest that white people should practice arrange marriage in their early 20s if white culture is to survive.

The Other White Girl would also be a perfect candidate for feminism, as feminism advocate their lifestyle as a religion. The universal attitude and soccer-mom behavior of The Other White Girl is very problematic for Asian-Aryanism.

Consider why any normal white person would want The Other White Girl more than an Asian one.

I use the shoe allegory. The rule is simple:

"We are attracted to people like ourselves. We are comfortable and feel free when our shoes fit us. Shoes outside our own realities cause us harm and anxiety. It is not a moral ethic to fit in other people's shoes."

White people feel comfortable around people like themselves. Different breeds of animals stay with their own breed because all breeds discriminate in favor of their own kind. This is a biological reality.

But this logic is quite a contradiction towards Asian-Aryanism, since there are two different breeds of people.

However, Asian-Aryanism argues that whites and Asians stick together, *in the same Asian-Aryan shoe!*

Our new evolutionary reality is between the two great races of whites and Asians. We prefer to stick our feet into these shoes because they improve our lives greatly. We cannot go and try to find The Other White Girl and abandon Asian-Aryanism, because she will eventually cause us pain. This issue has to be addressed within white culture. White women are problematic and have to be cured of their behavior. Asian-Aryanism promotes a whole new reality for a new shoe.

Now, a white person would argue that he should dump his asian "fetish" (a fun word used by racially-minded white people) and then try to find the needle-in-the-haystack that is The Other White Girl. This is sad irrational white/weeb nationalism. White people are gravitating towards Asians (and vice-versa) in large numbers because both sides are escaping the responsibilities of western society. Asian-

Aryanism seeks to improve the white condition through biculturalism.

We do not advocate white genocide. There can be whites, Asians, and Eurasians existing in the future all at once. White nationalists should try and find their sought after magical white girl and remake their own women as white-skinned Asians. Asian-Aryans will go our own natural route and create a culture that is Eurasian and avant-garde.

We are an alternative that is a solution to MGTOW and the verbally abusive creatures we call white women. She may redeem herself by becoming an Asian-Aryan, a weeb nationalist, or The Other White Girl.

4-4-17

4chan's Asian Fetish

Does 4chan have a fetish for anime characters and Asian women?

I am not a 4chan user. For a long time, I was a YTMND user. Today is the 8th birthday of my established name "pilleater." On April 9th, 2009, I created the username to spam my very own "Mr. Krabs" sites. I used Photoshop to cut out the head of Mr. Krabs and paste it on any average picture I could find through Google search.

I captured the sound from an annoying video I found while surfing Youtube. It's now quite famous. I spammed so much of the site, that the fad launched into the well-known "Oh I'm Mr. Krabs" meme that we know today. Even YouTube user Behind The Meme cited my first YTMND sites as the earliest origin behind the Mr. Krabs meme.[4] I take pride that I am an original meme creator.

But now the YTMND days are over. It's a dead website ruled over by no one. 4chan is still alive. Memes are being created everywhere, every week, and out of nowhere than relying on one single website. Some memes try to be esoteric to keep out the normies.

---

4 https://www.youtube.com/watch?v=bFQ66C2VXSM

4chan has always been a hotspot for weeb culture and anime nerds. I never was the person that hung out on a 4chan board. 4chan users are now trying to fit in with normie culture while being cutting-edge nerds at the same time. I really don't know what is real anymore.

The Anime Right was started as a meme to get 4chan zealots onto the Alt-Right. However, much of their culture is borrowed from the decadent culture of 4chan. Both the readers of 4chan and The Anime Right tend to be isolated, stay-at-home, bumfuck-midwest white kids that are starving? Strained? from working at a 711. It's a sad culture.

This crass behavior has skewed the ideology of 4chan into "trolling." The behavior that originally started from both *Something Awful* and *Encyclopedia Dramatica*. Now the scene has become terribly normie. Virtual reality has now succeeded physical reality.

The Anime Right, as defined by one of their admins Triggerbait, are "Nazis that like anime." Basically, the anime fan club of *The Daily Stormer*.

This behavior is ignorant to the fact that these so-called Nazi LARPers refuse to appreciate Asian culture. I have explained this in my previous article, "Getting 'The Anime Right' Out of The Alt-Right Bag."

91

Anime today is also perceived to be liked by the lower classes. At one point in time, "anime," in the English speaking world was unknown. A small niche of westerners appreciated the medium and thought highly of it. Now the medium is highly saturated with English dubs and translations of everything that can sell. "Anime" that can be sold in the Western world.

Manga and anime like *Patalliro, Aim for The Ace!, Cooking Papa,* and *Hell Baby* is extremely underground. Recently, *JoJo's Bizarre Adventure* has been enjoying some air time in the West.

The market likes to introduce cherry-picked animes upon the ignorant class of white consumers. Consumer culture is its own reality. A land of isolation and depression.

This is where the "fetish" comes in. By definition, a fetish is a type of abnormal sexual desire forced upon an object. Personally, the word "fetish' has been used by the liberal establishment to put blame and guilt upon white people when they want to be with people that enlighten their lives. Ironically, the only way to get rid of a fetish is either to stop thinking about the object or adapt a "normal" sexual code. Either the reformed person becomes a "nu-cuck" or a white nationalist.

There is no concrete answer towards "curing" a fetish. If we were to properly understand the word, a fetish could be treated as a disorder.

Most of the neckbeards and nerds that hang around 4chan, are disenfranchised white males. They talk about shock-art, Nazi politics, and autistic logic. However, whenever it comes to porn, they prefer to masturbate to pictures and videos of anime/hentai or Asian girls. They treat these things as sexual objects. But will any of these downtrodden people prefer to marry an Asian woman?

If they follow their bumfuck destiny and marry a bitchy feminist, or "That Other White Girl," their loyalties are still with their own race. Therefore, the anime and Asian girls were just used as sexual fantasies to get-off their perverted desires. This is where the insult of "fetish" comes in.

I am concerned about the future of these boys who are isolated and glued to a computer screen. I believe they can all become candidates for Asian-Aryanism.

When I first made my introductory Asian-Aryan video a while back, 4chan had a discussion about it. I gladly took the time and responded back to each of their replies. There are many answers to 4chan's Asian fetish.

First, let them jerk off to anime and Asian girls.

The argument for Asian-Aryanism will keep progressing. Why would they want to jerk off to "3D" porn or white girls? They know that these girls cause them harm. Boys feel safe when they imagine their sexual partner to be an anime character or Asian girl. They will eventually develop a future preference towards girls with Asian characteristics.

It may also seem that masturbating to their fetish is denigrating Asian girls as sexual objects, destroying the integrity they might for them as individuals (and ruining their chances to be with one). I don't think this should be a problem at all because most normal guys feel guilt after masturbation. But a strong man can overcome his sexual guilt. Strong men don't feel guilt after masturbation. Sexuality should be the moving factor towards finding a woman like oneself. Imaging an Asian girl with her clothes off when you see one out in public is a normal thing. She is still a potential candidate when you talk to her (you're just imaging if she can give you good head or not).

Second, these boys need to open about their love for Asian culture.

This may be expressed through weeb nationalism or even associating with The Anime Right. However, there are big problems when they are explicit white-advocates and anime aficionados at the same time. Their loyalties are mixed up. Again, the fetish accusation can be pointed directly at them. You can still love white people AND love Asian people too.

94

Asian-Aryanism is a safe space for that. These nerds really want a domineering and powerful Asian woman in their lives to change it around. Being loud and proud about Asian culture shows a devotion within a man. Asian-Aryanims is merely giving these confused boys words and meanings to be open about their true love.

Finally, the message has to be controlled. Fetish shaming is not going to lead someone to the Asian-Aryan side.

Cindy Young at Amped Asia wrote a few old articles titled *"8 Dating Mistakes You're Making with Asian Women"*[5] and *"Why Do White Guys Love Asian Girls So Much? A History of Yellow Fever."*[6] These petty arguments miss the point that men are careless. Young assumes men should "step up their game" and become something like Roosh V (even though she would be horrified at such a guy).

Hell, she even sounds like Aaron Cleary when he made a video about Asian-Aryanism.[7]

---

5 http://www.ampedasia.com/article/8-dating-mistakes-asian-women/

6 http://www.ampedasia.com/article/white-guys-asian-girls-history-yellow-fever/

7 https://www.youtube.com/watch?v=bGLw3Qml1H8

These civic-nationalist arguments will not work. Political-correctness and sucking down to women isn't the answer, it's the problem.

The Asian-Aryan message has to get out to these nerds. Their actions determine their ideology. They may bitch and forgive in the future and say "*yeah... I was in a dark place, I am so sorry,*" but that does not cut it. Being unapologetic and honest is a good ethic.

Let the jerks know that Asian-Aryanism is a path towards enlightenment and truth. The truth is white men prefer to be in the company of Asian women in today's post-liberal climate. Give them this truth, and 4chan will start leading the meme wars alongside Asian-Aryanism.

Asian-Aryanism has huge potential to become the next meme. It's a meme based upon the truth.

Having a "fetish" should not be shamed. Those who don't know themselves need to understand their own nature first. The enemy is someone who is inauthentic and dishonest about their own nature. It upsets me when whites flirt with Asian culture, and then fail to make devotional ties with the culture (fail to marry an Asian, or treat their interest in Asian culture as a "phase"). I feel that there is a lot of useless white people into Asian culture for SWPL reasons they are not aware of. If they truly were aware of their own behavior, they wouldn't be watching anime the way I watch it, or going to cosplay events. Whites must be honest with their own intentions. Otherwise, it's materialistic, consumer culture nihilism.

A confused person does not know what he truly wants. Does he want white culture? Or does he want anime? An Asian-Aryan gladly accepts both and synergizes the two. It's not a choice between one or the other, but a new standard that accepts both.

I would be happy to accept any 4chan nerd with open arms onto the Asian-Aryan side. So as long he is "yellow-pilled" about his own activities and sees the light of the rising sun.

4-5-17

The Proud Beta Male

How many times have you heard that "the beta male" is a dweeb and that "the alpha male" fucks all the pretty girls? The Chateau Heartiste tradition of "game" has grown into a discipline over the past decade. F. Roger Devlin's famous 2008 essay *Sexual Utopia in Power*, helped stabilized and create the Manosphere we know today. Society is decadent, yet, "red-pilled" white men are willing to work with it and become total douchebags like Roosh V.

The alpha gets the most sex, and the beta is the passive loser that get nothing because he's too weak to become the rapist.

But how come there are so many Americans that are considered "beta" today? Only a few are actually "alphas." Everyone wants to lift weights and get a body like The Golden One. Alphas are the douchebags that read *Return of Kings* and betas stay at home and watch anime.

…Great.

So why should betas even try and act like alphas?

I once had this discussion with Micheal Bell, who writes for Counter-Currents. He told me, "you've got to strive to become the alpha!"

I will admit the following:

I have been lifting weights in my personal gym and I have a steady diet. I sometimes get aggressive and talk about how I want to beat people up and what kind of? girls I want to have sex with. I jerk off to porn, and go to church on Sunday. I enjoy going out once in a while for a special event, whatever that may be (at an art gallery, a concert, a convention, a meet-up club, or eating out with a date).

But take into consideration that I am not an alcoholic (I would rather drink when I am near girls or with a special friend), I don't swear in my speech, I groom myself to look good, and I care about other people.

You can call me gay (since I tend to write and talk about the male aesthetic), but it's not like that at all.

I am not an extroverted meathead with a "bro" past. I am proud to say that I am a nice, honest, good and handsome beta male.

Again, not to sound "gay," but I like hanging out with aesthetically pleasing guys who are authentically good people. I believe in the Männerbund.

I have read Jack Donovan's *The Way of Men* and *Androphilia*, and understand the culture of the male instinct. Men flock with men they prefer to be with.

In no way am I shaming "Donnie," "Tony," or "Vinny," who work as manly plumbers and are what the gay community would call "daddies" and "bears." (Fucking gross, I'm not into that).

I like a certain type of guy that I grew up around. I don't like jerks who are obsessed with "scoring" and acting like wiggers. I appreciate the men who are in the military and the asexual athletes who care less about girls. You may be thinking I really must be a closet gay for talking like this. That's because I love all handsome men that sacrifice their lives to be male role-models and good beta guys.

Not everyone playing sports or holding a gun in the military are alpha. Most of them are betas (probably because they follow the rules).

I will agree that most gays are possibly confused betas. But most people who charade with the "gay" identity are really just confused people.

The best role models I had were guys with plaid shirts, into avant-garde electronic music, who had nice Asian girlfriends that cared about the family.

The family! This is the first thing I want to hear! That includes you!

In this atomized society, "game" is popular because everyone has high expectations. Aaron Clearey argues to *Enjoy The Decline* and follow a certain creed of *Bachelor Pad Economics.* However, this is leading towards a boring, fatalist life, with no real meaning.

Devlin has also argued that men should pick up the wisdom from Chateau Heartiste, *Return of Kings*, and Roosh V, even though you should ignore their "machiavellian sarcasm." Right?

The Manosphere and game culture corrupts men,[8] as Greg Johnson points out at Counter-Currents.

I am not a douchebag that strives to fit in with normies. In fact, I think my life is best summed up as *that weird hipster from that Asian Neo-folk band.*[9]

---

[8] https://www.counter-currents.com/2015/02/does-the-manosphere-morally-corrupt-men/

[9] Xiu Xiu

I like strange stuff. But I am also a good person. I'm not a spiteful Elliot Rodger trying to get revenge upon the world. I would even go so far to consider myself a "queer" in a world that doesn't't understand me.

A good beta role model is Ronnie Martin of the band Joy Electric. I follow his Twitter and listen to his sermons.[10] I love that guy to death and always try and emulate his behavior.

This "beta" behavior I am talking about is NOT bad at all! I believe being beta is a good thing. Being beta promotes good male characteristics. From being honest, submissive, creative, funny, average, caring, hardworking, dedicated, and just a plain *authentic* human being.

The alpha wants to make man into an intellectual, cultural thug. ...*Or a clever skinhead.*[11]

The beta is an honest man, like that old cartoon show, *Doug*.

Most Japanese men and their anime male counterparts, are natural betas. Sexy, submissive, and wonderful betas!

---

[10] His church in Ashland, Ohio is named after a famous New Order album.

[11] Jim Goad??

I love being a beta! Why should I feel shame that I am one? I love my body, I love my sex life, and I love what I do. I just wish I shared the world with other betas too. And when I say "betas," I am not talking about most normie losers.

I was (and still may be) a board game player, a pornography nerd, an edgy white nationalist, a sitar and chiptune musician, an alt-lit collector and writer, a high school cross-country runner, a gay model, and now (I am) open about my new adventure into Asian-Aryanism.

I believe Asian-Aryanism is close to the truth in this lying society. It's a path towards authentic happiness.

Now there can be an "alpha" Asian-Aryan (I would love that to happen). But let the truth be known, that all my Asian-Aryan friends are beta.

And they should not be condemned for being betas! Asian-Aryanism takes pride in the beta identity. It is the beta identity that matches so well with the Asian significant other and Eurasian offspring.

Being beta doesn't mean being a degenerate. A degenerate is an unhealthy and evil person that bows down to mainstream society.

They are the nu-cucks, and I HATE the nu-cucks.

Asian-Aryans are healthy people that have goals and dreams. They are good like Christians, and creative like the alt-right.

This life isn't about consuming and accepting the terrible fate of a mundane existence. Asian-Aryanism gives power to the enlightened, white American. Destiny is fulfilled when all are actions are authentic.

Again, why should we strive to become meathead alphas? Some guys are alpha. But we can't all be.

Both men and women have to understand the nature between the sexes. We can't just make up dreams and wish more from the other side.

Asian girls are fine with white guys being beta, and some quirky white girls like beta Asian guys (even delta).

I understand some of the gold-digging Chinese want more from their white men, or even some of the edgy Asian girls want to try black guys. There can be an acceptable form of "alpha Asian-Aryanism." ...But this should not be tolerated as our main motivation. We must respect each other's unique level of autonomy and strive for a loving community.

Big is always better, but authenticity creates culture. Asian-Aryanism is in the business of creating a future civilization.

I love being beta. I love beta guys and their kind Asian girlfriends.

5-1-17

I Love The Patriarchy!

I love the Patriarchy!

Yeah, you heard it, "I love the patriarchy!" Call me a sexist, even some intersectional crypto-racist, but I don't just love a single cis-patriarchy. No! I love the Asian-Aryan patriarchy!

I love it when white guys get with the quiet Asian girl romantically and I like it when Sexpat Losers post some AMWF stuff on my Twitter and fail to piss me off.

Am I some kind of cuck? No, I'm not. I like it when white girls act like anime characters or develop an Asian personality. And I like nerdy Asian guys who play StarCraft and make the crudest jokes ever. I feel like I belong with these people. It's a culture no one really wants to talk about. Yet, some of those artsy-fartsy people use to read Giant Robot magazine and now hang out by the dozen at Mitski shows. It makes me feel like I am in the same room as my brothers and sisters.

I'm a bicultural person. I'm not a multicultural person at all. I will listen to trap music with my Asian girlfriend and act hood sometimes. Okay, I can take *that* kind of culture from black people. Does it make me "diverse?" No, not really, I have my boundaries, and I choose to be with whites and Asians.

I love the biracial Asian-Aryan patriarchy! It does so many wonders!

White guys need to dump the type of white girls that act like Lena Dunham from ~~Mean~~ Girls, and get with the homely Asian girl that appreciates his time. Asian guys need to start reading Yukio Mishima and show white girls a post-Asian-American future away from toxic feminism. I'm such a nice guy, there could even be a yaoi Männerbund between white and Asian guys.[12] Call it gay, but I think that is progressive. A real patriarchy!

And for the girls? Let the Asian girls teach the white girls makeup tips on the train and let the white girls teach them how to be more Western.

I'm such a nice guy, I allow weebs to self-determine if they want too, and it's okay for me if Crazy Rich Asian girls want to move to Vancouver and have their Asian culture "whitewashed." I think all parties can agree they are in it for Asian-Aryanism.

---

[12] *Kaze to Ki no Uta* and *Patalliro!* are good examples of this.

107

Asian-Aryanism is not only a collective, a community, and a future race. It's also a spirit. Just like the "American spirit." Anybody can be an American if they pledge allegiance to the country, right? I don't want to kill the white or Asian races. I am giving a certain niche of people a space to grow. Asian-Aryanism supports big-entryism, and any white or Asian can come into the community at any time.

Asian-Aryanism is the best place to be a true hapa or Eurasian (whatever you want to be called). Both whites and Asians can agree upon having a Eurasian lover. A Eurasian person has two identities. While at the same time, everyone, White, Asian and Eurasian, has an Asian-Aryan identity.

…You know, Charles Murray who co-wrote *The Bell Curve* had an Asian wife? His theories about "the cognitive elite" are right. The high IQ elite will be Asian-Aryan.

It's okay if you want to be called either "white" or "Asian." I can agree, "Asian-Aryanism" is a low-brow term. …But it makes sense, yes?

If you are "white," or even change your mind and say you're "Asian," just like Roaming Millennial, aren't you both? Everyone faces challenges when they try and look for a third position.

So be it, you can have your Eurasian daughters and support the new white race. But again, there are opponents out there who are bigoted SJWs and egalitarian fanatics. That is not an Asian-Aryan value.

But I know you will be an Asian-Aryan too, that is, if you love the patriarchy in your own way.

…I love the patriarchy. It's what is going to create this new movement. Those nerdy, STEM white guys are going to have Eurasian kids and the next generation will be the ones open to Asian-Aryan culture. It's a matter of time before their kids try to considered themselves to be "Asian," and then they will reproduce with another white or Asian… or Asian-Aryan! I'm just waiting for the Asian-American guys to stand up and be vocal about being Asian-Aryan too.

And some Asian girls are now proud to be white too. …It's all coming together!

5-22-17

The Asian-Aryan Übermensch

Stop crying Asian guys.

Do you really want to embrace a victim mentality and call yourself "losers" in the multicultural game? Whenever you blame "whitey" for your problems, it's a sign that you really are weak. Not even Asian girls want to hear that from you.

You see, a lot of Asian girls are avoiding you because you don't have the white standards they grew up with. All you have to do is developed those same standards and approach them with ease. It's really easy. Most stable Asian guys know this. …It's just not talked about.

Why should "Asian-American" be another "minority" group of oppressed people begging for the white man to give them money? It's so easy to be the victim.

I don't believe Asian guys are losers at all. They are my close friends, and I would consider them brothers.

Ironically enough, you incel types like to brag about how righteous, justice, and beautiful an Asian Male / White Female couples are. I have no problems with the pairing. But you treat it as the *true* and honest form of an authentic relationship! (probably because there is no "white man" in it). I even hear arguments that children of a AMWF couple are MORE eugenically stable than children of WMAF.

...Are you SJWs that crazy to believe in such illogical reasoning? Both WMAF/AMWF come out just fine. It's a matter of the patriarchal position of the dad (*"ooooooo! did I say a bad word?"*).

Most guys want *their* culture first in the relationship. If the man is Asian, he wants to focus on the Asian side... If the man is white, most likely, a focus will be on the white side.

But this anti-white rhetoric has to go.

I am not anti-Asian. I am not in favor of white or asian genocide.

But again, why are you so triggered by the word "white?"

There is going to be a new type of Asian guy that is also proud to be white and a new type of white guy that will be proud to be Asian. This is the true nature of a bicultural experience.

Multiculturalism has given us global consumerism, rampant individualism, and a false sense of reality. People who keep up with this lie are not authentic. I strongly believe multiculturalism has given us more bicultural breakdowns– Whether you think that is a good thing or a bad one. Multiculturalism and "diversity" is a source of tension and conflict.

However, there is something genuine in a relationship that is bicultural.

There is a spiritual type of civil war within white people. And Asian people really don't care about it. It's like what's going to happen in *The Camp of the Saints*, where is civilization if all the white people are gone?

Asian men have to step up and become barbaric gentlemen. There is so much to admire of the appearance of an Asian man. He has a right to marry a white or Eurasian woman. I consider the couple both my brother and sister. He should consider the same when I pursue Asian and Eurasian women.

Oddly enough, I will get criticisms that "I am self-hating" and should embrace my "Asian" side.

Do you guys ever call out the double-standards of white guilt? I don't think so.

(...Or what about that awesome album, Dear God, I Hate Myself?)

I don't hate myself or anyone. I just want to be with people like myself. I hate people who force equality on me and ask for "gibsmedat." I can see through your lies and can spot an inauthentic person anytime.

Asian men shouldn't be the subjects of the weak. They have to stand up and help create an Asian-Aryan patriarchy.

I have said this many times, but imagine if you have five different types for groups working together:

1. White weebs (or "Asianized" whites) / WMWF.

2. "whitewashed" Asians / AMAF.

3. Eurasians (or Hapas) / EMEF.

4. Interracial parings of WMAF/AMWF/EMAF/AMEF/ WMEF/EMWF.

And 5, whites and Asians that want to fight for a new Asian-Aryan identity.

113

Now, let people from all five of those groups mingle and we can see true progress. All of them must be open about being an "Asian-Aryan," the same way an immigrant comes into America and says, "I'm a proud American."

This is what Asian-Aryanism is truly about. A new racial bond and understanding between whites and Asians.

You think we are some fringe "racist" group, when it is quite the opposite. We are trying to become a self-determined and aware people with our own little scene. We can have friendly allies. Most are misled, thinking we are evil.

Call us, the "post-Asian-American" group of people. We are red pilled, anti-SJW, and critical of liberal society. Even better, we are "Alt-Asian."

We have a unique culture that is a synergy of both white and Asian traditions. Some of us want to be the new "white" or "Asian-American" people, others see a third position. All can unite together to create something new, culturally in the arts, music, and blogosphere.

If you're an Asian guy reading this, great: we are very similar. We just prefer to be with people like ourselves. You *can* get an Asian, white, or Eurasian lover. We are looking out for your interest too. Just know that there are authentic white guys that want an Asian or Eurasian lover too.

Go beyond the SJWs and experience a new "yellow-pill."

Start reading Yukio Mishima and Arthur Schopenhauer, and admire the beauty of Eurasian women.

As men, we are in this together. You are my brothers, and we should love our sisters.

5-26-17

The Cult of The Extroverts

There is a problem with today's post-postmodern society. The divide of white people are not only based upon "the right kind of white people vs. the wrong kind of white people,"[13] but between introverts and extroverts.

Western society has reached a conclusion that the white man uses the Earth solely for his own resources. It's only there for him to exploit. Man is not dependent on nature, rather, Nature is dependent on him. So it is a long-term goal for Western man to consume and create "reason" within his environment. This has led to a negative downfall into nihilism.

Globalism, free-market capitalism, and individualism is based upon this empty and bleak nihilism. This has further created the culture we know as the "normies," filled with "chads" and "stacies." Chads and Stacies don't have the time to stay at home or work alone to create art, or even for that matter, contribute to something greater for society. Normies just want to go to the "bar" or go "clubbing" on the weekends and have sex with as many people as possible.

---

13 https://www.counter-currents.com/2010/12/smells-like-white-guilt-christian-landers-whiter-shades-of-pale/

116

Normies are so dangerous that they have created a new social standard based upon judging people if they are not "alpha" enough. The introverts have to stay home, play video games, surf 4chan, and continue a non-significant life based upon their own virtues that the normies forcefully condemn.

Ironically, it is the introverts that are creating the metapolitical and cultural foundation of our future society, while the extroverted normies are the consumers of the introverted dream. However, the introverts cannot participate in their own crafted dreams. The extroverts are the ones that role play their fantasies.

It is interesting that our American society praises those who participate in it. The values and ethics of a "participator" (a pre-socratic notion) are "alpha." It is confusing even more that American society is dominated by liberalism, and seeks to present a facade over everyone else with infinite nihilism and Sargon-of-Akkad-tier reasoning.

It is these "alphas" (the extroverted normies) that are successful in America. But the system lies and never presents, or even teaches, the issue of becoming the new barbarians. Not everyone can be an alpha. But there are desperate nerds and idiots that are so demanding to act and become some kind of "pussynerd." This is the cult of the extroverts.

Extroverts are not helping society; they are destroying it. I frown upon this childish behavior of, "*I am better than you because I have friends and do decadent things.*" It's true that the American man and woman has reached this level. The upper-class is decadent. Even worse is that the upper-middle-class wants to believe there is a stable aristocracy, when really they are lied too. Everyone is stuck in their social position, quietly suffering and being deluded with cognitive therapy. Only the upper-class has infinite freedom that the "American dream" begs people to believe in.

...We can't all be alphas.

It's foolish to think a man can transform into a Mishima-type in one day (besides, he will end up having emotional problem and doing something crazy).

I do believe in "self-improvement.'

I lift weights, I eat healthy, I take care of my body, and focus on my future. I want to be a good role model based upon morally good virtues. The disease of Western man is based upon excessive drinking, recreational drug use, casual sex, useless swearing, self-aware hip-hop references and pop-culture consumerism. This is unfortunately, for most white men, the only way to attract a disgusting female.

The introverts will even condemn each another for not being more extroverted! The cult of the extrovert is real because everyone wishes they were The New Barbarians... the supposed "winners" in life.

My problem with the alt-right is that it is becoming more normie and extroverted. Silly games of "going to the bar" and "drinking" does not move the cause forward. It's nihilism.

Idiot "gamers," furries, socialist, punk rockers, ...whatever proxy for nihilism, does the same thing to bond with other like-minded consumers. It's consumer-culture, plain and simple.

How many people are getting into these "queer" or "weird" movements and asking for the red-carpet treatment because they are special? Or rather, they are "an amazingly extroverted person?"

People like Based Stickman, Nathan Damigo, Emily Youcis, whoever hobbyist of being extroverted, ...not even contributing anything towards metapolitics, are indirect salesmen, selling the isolated introverts "hope" for the future.

How many LARPers came to that wall in New York City, to get on cam and "troll" that guy just to show how "cool" they were (*I mean, I was there too*).

119

For fucks sake, life is becoming more *scenester* than Mission Hill.

Try finding a date on Ok Cupid. All those women are spoiled with a glut of men to choose from! The sexual revolution liberated women's sexuality, not men's.

White women have been known to emulate the behavior of the genuine white man. They will go so far to role-play or even "cosplay" as a desire made up by the introverted.

…Harriet Sugarcookie calls her work "porn for geeks."

The introverted created Frankenstein's monster, –the extroverted class that runs society!

Percy Shelley also created a monster too when he wrote *Hymn to Intellectual Beauty.* That the "new woman" shall be based upon "intellectual desires" rather than the physical. …Now we have blue-haired SJWs that think they are living anime characters.

The cult of the extrovert is dangerous is because it's principles are based upon materialism. It's a competitive fashion statement, rather than a quest for authenticity, which introverts naturally struggle in life for. The cult of the extrovert is a creation of the introverted. The introverts like to dream alone in bed, *"if only my life was better and was like an adventure."*

What we think we know as "true virtues," have been destroyed by an extroverted and evil rapist. ...The innocent are being corrupted.

Everyone will judge me and say, *"Ha, well, are you going to be remembered in history if you stay at home and do nothing?"*

Again, this is something the cult of the extroverted would say.

In fact, a good example of the cult of the extroverted would be the very last passage of *Days of War, Nights of Love*, an anarchist lifestyle manifesto.

I won't quote it in details, but I will say that the narrator presents himself as a "truly free being that gets lots of sex and every day is an adventure."

...Western man is truly pathetic.

6-8-17

The Asian Feminist Fallacy

Imagine, if you will, an Asian girl growing up in America. She may be Chinese, Japanese, Korean, Southeast Asian, ...whatever, but she has a very similar background to most "Asian-American" girls growing up.

She grows up with her conservative or Americanized parents that want her to "get a job" and make $70,000 a year or more. She could be Eurasian, or that her parents are divorced. The parents may force upon her the values which are Asian in background, or they fail to see the undercurrents of the American society that she grows up with.

All her best friends are white. If she has other Asian friends, they are of her background, or they are Americanized like herself.

The "standard of beauty" for the American girl, is the typical "Stacy." She is a worshipping member of the cult of the extroverts, and she wants to grow up to be like Britney Spears or Lady Gaga.

Going on such dating platforms like Bumble, you will be bombarded with blonde, valley girls that are right out of college. Casually, they love to drink beer and hang around white "Chads." But talk about race with them, they will refuse to answer the question.

This is by default, the normie white middle-class nationalism that Matthew Heimbach wishes to awaken. Of course, most of these white girls are liberal, because they just don't want to offend anyone while they go to the bar every Saturday night.

Are normies a problem? Of course they are. People on the internet have a genuine hatred for them as they provide no contribution to society, but rather as working bee drones that dance in it when they are off from work.

Is this really "the standard of beauty" we are told by higher education and liberal academia?

Academia really wants the new globalized person to be something of a mixed-race character. The media and movie industry would like everyone high on drugs, and blissfully enjoying life, while they are robbed of their money every day. To be a good consumer is also to act like one. Even if all the consumers are Chads and Stacies (and they certainly will get offended if you call out football).

Imagine the deracinated Asian-American girl, growing up with her other white girlfriends. The other white girls know she belongs to a different race, but they treat her special because "she is Asian."

The truth is that people prefer to be with people like themselves. Every single race of people just doesn't want to

123

admit to those crucial facts. The same goes with telling your kids that Santa Claus is real and that "sexuality is not that important."

...Race and sexuality are real. But it's odd how our society has been re-appropriating, as well as trying to surpass, such natural urges.

Martin Heidegger argued that the only way humans can have a peaceful existence with one another is if we understand ourselves as animals, and are in tune with our limits. This requires an understanding of both racial and family background, the sexual urges we repress, and the social positions and identity we role-play. It's not an easy thing to do. That's why there was such a thing called The Frankfort School.

By the time any Asian-American girl is in her 20s, she has unrealistic expectations that she will marry a nice white Prince Charming, who will come to her aid and marry her at 23. Unfortunately, she might become like all the other bimbos, by sleeping around with chads and then questioning "why have none of them picked me up as a wife?" It obviously has something to do with "racism."

Now, for a white girl, this cannot work because whites are not a minority people. Anyone growing up in their mid-20s will start to realize that we are animals, and that race and IQ is real, and that we are all going to die.

And so, Little Ms. Asian-American girl becomes a feminist, not because she hates men, but because she hates how men don't treat her the same as white women.

It is incredibly ironic for the Asian feminist that she wants to abolish "patriarchy," when really it only refers to her Asian side. This will help increase her chance getting her a white husband.

There is a great fallacy in the Asian feminist argument that seems counterproductive towards Asian-Aryanism.

First, the argument is anti-white. The normie will have a liberal view of race, and assume that the decadent standard of behavior is also "the white beauty standard." They fail to see that some greater power, beyond the nature of white people, is manipulating all classes below the upper.

An Asian feminist of this type will hate "the white patriarchy" and yet want to belong in the same Urban Outfitters clique of other white people. She has an irrational hatred towards "white culture," yet ironically wishes to assimilate with it. It's one big distorted feedback loop.

Second, there is a very weak understanding of race relations. An Asian feminist just wants to be "just like everyone else" and will enjoy the same decadence everyone is getting. Of course, she hasn't realized that white nationalism and traditions are quite aware of the normie problem. She wants a declining party culture, while we want upward progress towards self-improvement. Egalitarianism is our problem.

Third, The Asian feminist is wrong for putting her trust with "the wrong type of white people," mainly, meathead jocks. She assumes that even the nerdy white guy with the STEM degree is exactly like a football jock. If she was being more traditional, read some books, and realized that being a thot is not a happy life, could she understand greater accomplishment and an authentic relationship. Her obsession with "white guys treat me as a sexual object," is bogus because she is enabling men to treat her as an object. The real white guys that want Asian girls, authentically, are considered to be Asian-Aryans.

And finally, she never considers the very idea that there are authentic white guys that do want to have an Asian wife. But both sides are too afraid to be vocal about their love is because they will get labeled as a "racist" and "pervert." There is no definite meaning or words that can help WMAF/AMWF Eurasian couples out.

The Asian feminist is both beneficial and a burden. She argues for a future Asian-Aryan society, but falls for the double standard of anti-white hatred and "multiculturalism." She wants to be the very white person that Christian Lander makes fun of in *Stuff White People Like*.

It may also be true that an Asian-American girl or someone who is Eurasian has it much harder, psychologically and socially. The cure for this is Asian-Aryanism. It is natural to belong with people like ourselves. There is no open environment for her to truly express herself as an Asian-Aryan princess.

But now, there is the internet.

Once the introverted and downtrodden Asian-Aryans will realize this, they will create an intellectual foundation that will lead IRL extrovert advocates fighting and being open about living the Asian-Aryan lifestyle. We must plant the seeds of the future.

The Asian feminist will come to our side. It's only natural for her to do so.

6-19-17

Get The Balance Right!

"Aww. Look at you. 25-year old Robert Smith just got his first job working for Verizon selling cable service. Every morning, he has to put on his suit and tie, check in at his little cubicle, talk about his so-called favorite sitcom by the water cooler, drive back home to his little shitty apartment, and get a kiss from his ugly little Asian girl. ...Isn't that wonderful?"

I don't like the left-wing, but there is some wisdom to Deleuze's *Capitalism and Schizophrenia*. The piece should have been considered "creative writing mixed with pseudo-academic pablum." Nonetheless, actual perverted and depraved aristocrats admire his work as the truth.

For Deleuze, our American capitalist society has created schizophrenia among what would be the normal and healthy person. The average person only cares for his own self-interest and uses the Earth as his never-ending resource. It is one big spiral down into decadent nihilism.

...But the normal person couldn't tell you this. The normal person is so brainwashed with Cultural Marxist ideas, that he couldn't even tell you why it's right to let refugees in the country. The New Left succeeded not in ideology, but in the culture war.

A failure in this society is an anti-capitalist. Take a look at the dirty AntiFa, the trust-fund professor, and barista radical, and the artist. The intellects, or the honestly good-natured people, suffer because they can't make income. The system punishes them for having a certain personality trait. Therefore, if one is to succeed in the market, one has to be a whore. Rather, a pre-socratic barbarian acting like a Socratic aristocrat.

Capitalism is a system made for Western people in the context of modernity. When whites rule the world, they bring along capitalism too. Everywhere is dominated with Coca-Cola and shopping malls. Are the nonwhites enjoying capitalism?

Rudyard Kipling proposed something in the "white man's burden." To paraphrase:

1. Should white people colonize the world in hope that nonwhites will leave their savage backgrounds, and break free into the world that is the western experience?

Or 2. Should white people protect and stay in their country, playing watch guard around the world and advocate ethnonationalism?

...Take on the white man's burden. There is no clear answer. It's twofold.

Meanwhile, other non-whites, like Asians, are cheating the system. They are fooling white men into deceitful tricks based upon values that clash with Western ones. Asians, especially the Chinese, wish to expand their empire by getting into positions of power and marginalizing Western people. The Chinese had to adapt to world capitalism in their own unique Confucius manner.

The typical New York and Californian liberal at a fast rate is interbreeding with Northeast Asians. Nick Land argued that this has something to do with "transhumanism" and a new alien-human race that will conquer the stars. Some of us call it "Asian-Aryanism."

Let's look back at the arrogant life of Robert Smith…

"Five years ago, Robert was a transfer student from New Jersey, and moved in as a Freshmen at a promising private Women's college (now accepting men for the first time). Here, he will get his Bachelors in Economics, and as well appreciate his love for the fine arts. Meanwhile, while being forced to hang out with other ignorant late teenagers and early 20 somethings, Robert meets the love of his life, Stacy, at a club gathering based upon video-games. They soon have to hug every morning before class begins, even kiss on some emotional dependency. Public Displays of Affection are frequent. They might sleep together in the same dorm. Then there is that one day, during sophomore year, they fuck for the first time. …And then it's off to doing a senior project about "Social Justice in the Jesuit

Tradition" for Robert, and Stacy? "Shakespeare and Wolfgang Iser." Really boring and programmable shit. They don't see each other in the summer. Yet Robert will make the occasional drive to see her. Rainbows and Unicorns! ...And now, both getting a BA in English and Communications (a supposed double major), they have to look for work. For the first time, life was about climbing a social ladder and hanging around with an organized playtime like it was school. Not anymore. Robert has to surf Craigslist for a place to stay and Indeed.com for a career. And what about Stacy? Her Chinese parents want her to succeed and assimilate with the "American Standard." She has a huge trust fund of $500,000. She could spend it on grad school, or put down the money and start a family. She chooses the latter. Now, little Robert and Stacy live out in the middle of bumfuck West Chester, Pennsylvania nowhere (without roots of their original states) and are having the "time of their lives" living together. 25-year-old Robert and 23-year-old Stacy. Give it two years, either they will have a kid, or divorce miserably. Cupcakes, Castles, and happiness forever."

…And you see, this trajectory has been happening with the normie for about three generations. White baby boomers had it so easy to live in the suburbs and have three children, now turned over to Gen-X families that work in cubicles and let their wife work in the same position. Now it's the millennials turn, and shit is reaching a tipping point.

Blogger Vincent Law is right, "we live in a post-normie society."[14]

Young men could only live the normie life by marrying the typical Chinese girl after his money. An Asian, "gibsmedat."

The truth is that Gen-X parents were behind this "Boomerang" effect. They had it planned out when they were experiencing youth. *"It's only best if my kids lived a better life than I did.* "And even to a racial extent, *"They are individuals! They can do what they want. Here is the money! Now go follow your dreams!"*

Typical spineless, white American parents.

Compare that to the Chinese family, *"Either you honor or disgrace us. But we can work it out if you marry into modernity."*

Robert has a big shit-grin on his face. He knows he has to **act** if he wants to keep Stacy. Stacy is only in it for the position of power and she fears complete boredom. It's only "natural" to move "up" and start a family at this age. Otherwise, you would have to suffer the nihilistic world of 9-5 work, liberal graduate school, or the void that is total

---

14 https://altright.com/2017/06/21/do-we-live-in-a-post-normie-society/

darkness. They both need something to role-play in order to avoid the struggle of the common man.

They never really were free.

They had to constantly "get the balance right."

Just like that classic Depeche Mode song.

"And you thought this was going to be good, right? Isn't life wonderful? You're a suit-and-tie dependent indirect salesmen to a wife that doesn't even look like you? You're in debt and not so sure how long you are going to pay off the college you sold your youth to, for the only reason that you could lose your virginity and be a man? Was it even that much in the long run? And this girl you met, you could have ignored her and moved back into your parent's house, but you insisted "she was the one" and now you are roleplaying a character you watch in cartoons and movies. 25-years-old. Are you really an adult? Or are you a simulacrum of the new man that capitalist society wants?"

Robert and Stacy both have schizophrenia. They are in denial about it. No values or honest people ever told them that this life is inauthentic. Any second now the lie can pop and they will break up. They can always keep going, so as long they "get the balance right."

133

There's more besides joyrides

Little house in the countryside

Understand, learn to demand,

Compromise, sometimes lie

Be responsible, respectable,

Stable but gullible

Concerned and caring, help the helpless

But always remain ultimately selfish

You think you've got a hold of it all

You haven't got a hold at all

When you reach the top, get ready to drop

Prepare yourself for the fall, you're gonna fall

It's almost predictable

...Get the balance right!!

6-22-17

Shhh! Freemasonry!

"...it is really not appropriate to tell someone's real name to others without their permission if they are using a pseudonym. Please do not do this to me or anyone else again." -An IRL Homonationalist.

...If you hang out in an urban liberal city, and you once were an art student hanging out at punk rock shows, chances are you have met an eccentric person. I met a Jehovah's Witness into avant-garde noise music, an Asian porn actress who is sympathetic to my views, an openly gay white nationalist, AntiFa trannies, and shock art beatniks.

They all have something in common. ...They don't want to get "dox."

Everyone in this post-post modern society has a profession, whatever that is being a music teacher, working for Verizon, selling soft drinks, or the guy that repairs TVs, at least one of these professions has some type of "weird" or "queer" type of personality. If the boss ever found out about their decadent activities, they would be fired, simply because the business doesn't want one person to reflect the compacts public-relations image as a whole.

Hell, imagine if Christian Weston Chandler got a job working for Sega!

Once they have no job, they can't spend their money pursing the "revolution" or the decadent things they love doing on the weekends.

Look at Johnny. What a nice guy who goes to church every Sunday. Turns out he sucks dick and he's into white nationalism!

Ahh, little Suzy. Straight A+ student at this American university! But on Fridays, she's a singer in hardcore punk band and a camgirl on the side!

And little Jimmy, the quiet guy who works in IT. Yeah… he loves cocaine and into furry fandom!

…and they call that avant-garde culture?

They all belong to the same cult of extroverts and slide down the path of decadent nihilism. Would you want a comforting lie? Or an unpleasant truth?

"And here we have the Anti-Fascist Action! Everyones favorite superheroes! They don black and fight against this repressive system! You can't see them. Because they are all from the internet! They are one!"

137

…not even the good guys fighting for social justice want to be doxed!

I'm telling you, no one wants to get doxed in the year 2017. Everyone wants to go to the bar and shut the fuck up. No one is willing to take greater responsibilities by going out in public.

Even worse is that all these *Mission Hill*, *Portlandia*, or Urban Elf caricatures have one thing in common. Each have their own secret club one has to enter. Be it on a Discord sever or a punk show playing in some "cool guys" basement.

It's petty like that old Bernstein Bear's book, "*No Girls Allowed.*"

No Normies Allowed.

No Cucks Allowed.

No Fascist Allowed.

No Fags Allowed.

No Cisgendered Men Allowed.

No Blacks Allowed.

No Whites Allowed.

No Jews Allowed.

No Newfags Allowed.

…Shit. What's not allowed? People draw their boundaries and create their own physical narratives about life. Everyone has their own personal bubble, or "safe space." We lost the sense of a greater collective, in favor of extreme individualism and global consumerism. Where is the good life?

But what makes me the most agitated as I watch America burn to the ground, is that some 20 to 30 something year old bearded hipster is going to tell me that I have to "do" certain things to be "accepted" by his equally urban elf friends.

…Club routines include going to the bar, picking up thots, and talking about X. (X can be the alt-right, anime, music, critical theory, religion… anything).

This "Shhh! It's a secret" Freemason club is utterly pretentious.

They tell you it's for your own security, when really, no one gives a shit. Then they say "no one understands us" when you should just approach someone without fear. And then they say "we are an elite group of people" when really they are just roleplaying as the victim.

Cops, lawyers, politicians, journalist, musicians, artist, professors, and any contribution-to-society-profession are public figures!

There is something weak about a man that hides behind a mask. Lenny Bruce puts on a "performance" and did not reflect the person who he was… though you could argue, his expression was his creation. I use the name "pilleater" as a way to express pilleater's thoughts.

…so the story goes of Dr. Jekyll and Mr. Sam Hyde!

A man who hides, fears death. Death is coming closer every day of my life. I think about the double digit age where I am. Age always matters every day of my life. One day, I will be 88, or 92, or older, and my body will break down. We are all going to die one day. Be prepared for it the next day.

Decadent nihilism has erased the thought of death. Everything is just a "phase" so we can enjoy 2017-2037, the next twenty years of our youthful existence! *The years of our lives!*

This feeling of belonging to a "secret underground club against a tyrannical and oppressive system" is wishful thinking. It's a delight for those who consume off of it. If pre-socratic notions result to "I just want to get laid every week and watch anime until I die," then it is the problem. Decadent, hedonistic, materialistic nihilism is the problem.

And to make it all relative, someone is always in a club YOU can't enter! Always in a club or political party that results to normie behavior with the side of a perverted interest.

Donald Trump won the election because he came out of the closet. There was no freemasonry.

...It was rather esoteric meme magic that go him in.

Millennials want to believe they are fighting against the system. They want to use their internet names IRL, while being scared shitless if someone found out about their powerword.

...It's like what pedophiles do. They don't say, "yeah I fuck little boys," they rather say, "BL."

No contribution of society is being made from this silly freemason game.

I believe in performance art. We put on masks and act certain ways to express ourselves as an artist. That fake name is attached to our real self, and eventually, we will come out of the closet too (in fact, you should do it now).

Has any serial killer actually gotten away in history? These freemasons believe history will be written without them! (and they can still go to the bar on the weekends and pick up their favorite thots).

I don't give a shit if you call me Francis. I like that. You're real fucking close to me if you do. If you call me Joey and you're a cute girl, I will be your guy. And when you call me "pilleater," you're talking to my ego.

I respect someone's privacy, but if you're going out doing normie things… well, expect to be "doxed" and be treated as a normie.

The water is fine! Think about what Milo has done to himself. Even Based Stickman. …Sacrifice.

I think of myself as a martyr. I am doing this for myself. This is who I am. I am a growing man eager to act as a professional and represent myself when confronted with a situation. I take all responsibility.

Say all you want that "it's for our own protection," at least be an adult and suffer.

"Consent culture" is making a comeback as "please don't say my powerword because it hurts my feelings / or I am too cool for you" consent culture.

This pretentious "secret Freemason club" has got to go. For one, it tells me your either criminal in behavior, or trying to belong in the **Kool Kids Klub.**

The KKK. …That sounds so familiar.

7-2-17

Motivated by Self-Hatred?

Some have said that Asian-Aryanism is motivated by a self-hatred against one's own people and rather renews a loving feeling towards the other.

It might be true that every young White millennial boy wants to have an Asian girlfriend because he is sick and tired of the decadent behavior of the White girl. And it could be said that Americanized Asian girls hate Asian men because they are nothing like empowering and creative White men.

And then there is White girls hating on White guys and Asian guys hating on Asian girls. Obviously, such trends, mean that Asian-Aryanism is based upon self-hatred.

Not exactly.

Peggy McIntosh wrote *White Privilege: Unpacking the Invisible Knapsack* as a cutting-edge piece of academic literature to instill altruistic self-hatred among white liberals. Today, you see normie whites believe in "white guilt" so they can make other non-whites shut-up while they go do their white people things.

The same is true about Asian feminism. However, Asian-Aryanism is open and honest. We are not hiding anything from anyone. We are White, Asian, and Eurasian people that want to mix our genes together. Eurasian people will have a higher sense of aristocracy, but we are opening the entryist doors to our white and Asian parents.

The individual, like an "American," has a certain level of autonomy they practice as a devoted Asian-Aryan. This isn't "pathological altruism," but a new religious, cultural, and lifestyle path to fight against the nihilistic society we have today.

We "hate" because we are motivated to draw lines. We put up a barrier against the opponents that don't want to hear us. Johnny hates Sarah because she is a thot.

It is more in Johnny's interest to live his life with Atsuka. It may be true that Atsuka loves white culture, yet doesn't know how to be a part of it. So she will marry Johnny. And then Stephanie marries Kurt (Korean guy) and Kurt wants to be "Americanized." And their children will also be looking for others interested in their own White and Asian background.

This is the start of a new culture (and race) of people that would like their own self-determination rather than the confines of "White" or "Asian."

Are they motivated by hatred? Of course not. They hate liberal society and everything that promotes materialism, hedonism, decadence, and nihilism.

Plato once wrote about a androgynous race of people in *Symposium*. A mega race that once ruled before humanity. French avant-garde thinker Micheal Foucault wrote in *The History of Sexuality* that this mythic proto-race of people were the true intellects of society. Therefore, it was a mission in Foucault's life to create a new tranny Männerbund group of people that would rule over academia.

Foucault's dedication to the creation of the androgynous race has been quite successful. But ironically, it has instilled a "beta" level of the "game hierarchy" that rules over us. Foucault only wanted the beta to be in charge of everything. This naturally cannot work.

The internet has swept away all the useless information of the French school of so-called "deconstruction" and has put the artist "posing-as-an-academic" to shame. There are pseudo-scientists, and Foucault is one of them.

This post-postmodern society rewards certain personality traits in this far-left-leaning Anglo-Saxon capitalism. It punishes those who are naturally healthy, good, and abiding. Only the ugly are being rewarded with the best.

This institution is spreading dysgenics at the top and repressing eugenics at the bottom.

The strong, Christian white boy is being depleted of his female companion. The white girl has high expectations of life and is further pursuing the decadent men at the top. This is resulting in a declining rate of white birthrates.

Does the innocent man have to read Roosh V's *Bang* in order to pick up a decent woman? To play the "game" Roosh advocates is Neo-Darwinism. Our liberal society argues we are free to do what we want, and selfishly rewards those who are at the top. A soft genocide is happening to the virtuous.

We don't have to become male-thots like Roosh in order to woo white women. We just have to be yellow-pilled on the subject.

It took time for liberal society to get their non-gender beta male intellectual to run the institutions. To live the good life, we have to find it, even if it's hiding under a rock. We don't have to change our personalities and become like Jack Donovan. We surf towards the people who are willing to accept the good life. White and Asian people have created a cultural bridge in the past century. This union is the only way to escape the rotten society we call "multiculturalism." People prefer to be with people like themselves.

If Asian-Aryanism had one wish upon society, we would want to live in a culture where everyone is a Final Fantasy character. We would make anime real.

...Asian-Aryanism is about love, not hate. We naturally love our people and hate those who try and stop us.

The nerdy guy who plays *Magic: The Gathering* can be himself around the fat Chinese girl he met in high school. The strong White guy and his thot-wannabe Asian girl have a place to stay. And the mid-twenty something who lives with his parents feels liberated when he meets up with his Asian lover on the weekends.

We are against Anglo-Saxon capitalism and the nihilism it has produced. When you are yellow-pilled, a new light will shine upon you. A new standard to be yourself will be accepted.

Don't worry about trying to "game" girls or constantly hate on yourself to woo others. Like Foucault's magic race of trannies, we are the new race of people from the times before the *Symposium*.

We are motivated by aesthetics, the good life, and our Asian-Aryan future.   *7-8-17*

STEM Supremacy

During my senior year of college, I took a big black pill. That pill was Aaron Clarey's book *Worthless*. Clarey argues that the liberal arts degree is "worthless" (in the economic sense) and that pursing a STEM degree (Science, Technology, Engineering, and Math) was more valuable. A STEM degree could land you a job right out of college.

This, he argues, is because there is a high consumer demand for people to create/regulate technology. While this may seem ideal, unfortunately, Clarey also argues that the economy is unpredictable, and if a comet came crashing down on the earth and killed every single English speaker, the man with an English degree would become the new millionaire.

I do believe there is a rise in members of the upper-middle white class pursing STEM degrees because their Gen-X parents have arts degrees (hardly anyone went to college in the 80s).

The current fad is that the liberal arts degree, which may be English, Psychology, Political Science, Sociology, or Fine Arts, is an anti-money-maker for the millennial generation. There is a prudish, conservative, and typical mid-west arrogant attitude of white people that pursue STEM degrees, simply because "that's what makes money."

149

This leads to something of a "STEM supremacy" which bashes on the unstable nature of undergrad education, and belittles those students who pursue an arts degree. It has never occurred to these people that there were students who entered college because they wanted an "Asian Studies" degree. Passion and determination does not correlate with them.

I had a prissy conservative girl tell me these things that my "English and Communication" degree was worthless because "no one wants it." In addition, she told me that ANYONE can teach in Japan and that requiring a "bachelor degree" for it is a scam. This did offend me. Being drunk, I scoffed her off quickly (I found out she had a boyfriend) and told her why it's meaningful for some people.

She had a quick rebuttal, "You always talk about this Asian thing. Please! I don't want to hear it again!" (When I met her, I had just got done with my first public speaking event. I got drunk beforehand and rambled on about why the world belongs to Asians. She still doesn't know what I do online).

She had to walk away from my input. After all, she did criticize me, because I didn't understand that is has to do with "parenting, not race." (a sign of her morally upright and affirmative cryptic-white nationalism).

...A few days earlier, I was trying to practice game with a friend at a sips event. I was shocked to find that all the men and women were overwhelming white, blonde, and in their late 20s and 30s. And all worked in the same cubicle jobs with their STEM degrees!

Within five rejections, I heard the same stuff over and over again from the same type of white girl (I went to X school, I make 60-80 a year doing X, we are going on vacation to the island of X). This upper-middle class group of white people is embarrassingly shameful. All of them live their lives like they are still in high school, yet work mundane jobs to keep the system afloat for their decadent behavior.

Clarey, who also wrote a book *Enjoy The Decline*, argues that you should get a good-paying job and do what you want with your time. ...This professional nihilism, is celebrated by Clarey!

The STEM supremacists like to think they are the holy ones that made "the right choice" with their lives. When ironically, all they do is compete to live in the same obnoxious, SWPL lifestyle as their peers. This has unfortunately made a further divide between "The right kind of white people," vs. "The wrong kind of white people."

The Rights, who are the STEM supremacist, verse The Wrongs, or the chumps that spend their money and do what they want. This spiritual war still rages on for white people.

As an American person of mixed European descent, I should have naturally become a STEM supremacist! But instead, I got my degree in "English and Communications" because I was passionate about it (And really, all I ever wanted was to get my degree in Asian Studies).

There were obvious "choices" for me to go the route of STEM. I did take many math, computer, and chemistry classes. Bit in the end, it never satisfied me.

Both of my parents come from a culture of washed-up chads and stacies. Both of them never went to college, and I am happy that I was able to get a debt-free college education. I pursued my dreams, not my income.

As a white person with this social privilege, I am grateful to have a trust fund, a pool in the backyard, two dogs and a cat, hardware synthesizers, and a fine art collection. ...Now the STEM supremacist would say to me, "It was your parent's fault for not parenting you in the right direction!"

Again, we have this ongoing war between the Rights and the Wrongs. Upper-middle class white people are still bitching about other white people they are afraid to associate with.

I am a musician, a blogger, an artist, and a full-time NEET that does what I love to do. ...Eventually, I will get "the job" and income to support myself and bigger projects.

...Although, like everyone else, I do wish I had better guidance in my life.

But these STEM supremacists are no different from their thot counterparts.

You know, I might become an established artist in the future with an income. With that, I can work at most jobs. I also have the opportunity to teach overseas (most normies can't do that). And I am proud of my own educational background!

The problem today is that the education system is destroyed because no one wants to put "value" on degrees anymore. The value for an English degree is neglected because it is overruled by ideology and shitty jobs at Barnes & Nobles.

Those who hold arts degrees either go back to university to spend more money to match their STEM supremacist peers (which is a shock for the upper-middle class white girl who pursues English) or simply, make up a lie that their degrees have the same STEM value. Both these choices are obviously wrong.

153

I hate normies. I never wanted to be like a normie. ... Normies ruin everything!

Only a selected few belong in college. A degree is a personal accomplishment, not a societal one.

A "college degree" is a rite-of-passage for the common white person. Imagine, someone of the age between 20-22 receives a college education and now has to make sense of the outside world. As I wrote before, imagine being 25 in the undergrad college... they will never let you in! The undergrad education has become an expensive high-school / teenage daycare center. This is a dangerous problem with millennials.

As a dedicated person for the Euro-Asian cause, Chads and stacies cramp my style. I take pride I went to college and learned how to write and speak Japanese (はい). But I don't take pride that I go to the bar and hang with STEM supremacist.

...I would rather hang out with other Asians or Euro-Asians with "worthless" degrees.

7-19-17

Introducing The Alt-Left

There is a lot going on in the news about the "alt-left." Donald Trump said it as a joke during a conference, and there is also a crazy website named, "Alt Left Watch." (I won't link it because it is too crazy). The only publication to get it right was from *The Week*:

"As best I can tell, the very first people to use the term "alt-left" was a tiny faction within the alt-right, who favor more left-leaning economic policy. However, this did not catch on. The actual popular use came later, from two sources, more or less simultaneously. First was a quote from mainstream Republicans, desperately looking for something to distract from the fact that their party was now headed by an elderly addle-brained racist. If the left also had racists, then it somehow wasn't so bad that Republicans had nominated one for president."[15]

The alt-left is indeed a tiny faction, and I believe the only person willing to be the ultimate judge on the issue is Brandon Adamson. However, if an "alt-left" scene is to grow, then it can't fall under the same corrupted and immoral nature of the current "left-wing" we have today.

---

[15] http://theweek.com/articles/718721/troubling-origins-trumps-altleft-smear

As of right now, I denounced the alt-right after the failure of the Unite the Right rally in Charlottesville. It's no longer about queers associating with Boyd Rice or Death in June, it's a cluster-fuck of misguided LARPy teenagers and intersectional "identitarians." The latter group is hostile towards Asian-Aryanism. Furthermore, it is now "cool" and "hip" to be a tumblr chick and say you are "red pilled."

As I said before, the Kool Kids Klub are responsible for this, and each individual is guilty of whoring themselves to be "cooler" than the next. I won't name names, but I know some of these asshats. Next time I see any of these Kool Kids, I'm going to fucking destroy them.

…But Kool Kids are everywhere. White kids from the ages of 17-28 are responsible for such hipster douchebagery. And the coming tide of "the alt-left" is no exception. Now, I am not saying I am not guilty of such hipster culture (I do jokingly promote it through my social media and this website). However, we are fighting for metapolitics, and the current metapolitical tide is with the misguided white and Asian youth. Whoever wins this intellectual discourse on the internet, creates the obnoxious punk-house-party kids we see in every urban and metrosexual city.

Asian-Aryanism plants the seeds in all areas, introverted and extroverted. There will be Asian-Aryan Chads and Asian-Aryan Virgins (if you want to use that terminology). And there will be less hostility towards this peaceful movement that prefers to be with people like themselves in an age of post-liberalism and multiculturalism.

The youth of the alt-right is foolish to consider throwing their opponents into gas chambers and making excuses like "I'm gay and I'm just like you." This will only further divide the alt-right as "nazies" and create an entire new generation hostile against them. It's why there needs to be a new focus on an alt-left movement.

This alt-left movement will not be the decadent "left-wing" or "antifa" we know from our culture. The alt-left will have a concrete foundation in these golden rules:

1. The "left" is a western experience. It is not compatible with non-white civilizations, and is rather a "term" to describe the interest of the people and their own liberty. It is suggestive rather than definitive.

2. The alt-left is a trinity about **friends, family**, and **freedom**. The alt-left fights for universal friendship, whoever we may associate and live our lives with. The alt-left will protect our families, private or public, and will advocate natural order of both the patriarchy and matriarchy along with tradition. And the alt-left will fight for "freedom," the desire we feel as human beings that wish to transcendent the boundaries of human nature. We are not transhumanist and feel that it is immoral to be so. For obvious reasons: take a look at the stupid fad of transgender rights and "the progressive stack."

3. The alt-left is starting over again at year zero. Everything we knew as a "left-wing" will be destroyed. The French Revolution was a misunderstanding, communism goes against human nature, and The Frankfort / New Left school is wrong (and a slow defeat for the left to give up and create "Cultural Marxism"). We don't associate with Žižek, Derrida, Foucault, Althusser, Deleuze, or any kooky "postmodern" philosopher that is talented in rhetorical, pseudo-scientific, creative writing. It is important that the alt-left is critical of everything the left stands for, and creates a new culture and institution beyond what we know as the "the transhumanist mind virus." The movement will be peaceful and voluntary.

4. The alt-left is not about "social justice," "progress," or "equality." The alt-left is against egalitarianism, root and branch. Equality is not a good, and is a complete ideology of its own that is often mistaken by a normie as "the left." The alt-left will be completely removed from egalitarianism and focus on friends, family, and freedom in their own right.

5. The alt-left will not be hostile against the right wing. It will however be critical of the trad-fetishization and the close-minded conservative issues they radically uphold, but the alt-left is about ending the spiritual war between "left vs. right." The alt-left wishes to create a movement that is against dictionary definitions. There are too many normies that associate with "the left," and spread "cultural marxist" values. They don't even know what side they are on.

6. The alt-left is planning for a future after multiculturalism, diversity, and the postmodern world. It believes that "ethnonationalism" is a possible surrogate and cure for egalitarianism and The Kalergi Plan (the alt-left is against this program as well). The alt-left is acting as a responsible parent and gambling on a future that is distant and away from the pozzed society we suffer through now.

...These are some points what the alt-left should stand for. If only we had more bloggers advocating for such a movement, we could have more peace and less violence in today's racial and political climate. But again, the spiritual divide between left and right still conquers us as a people. Our common enemy is the globalist that wants to erase our identities. We want to be with people like ourselves and have our own cultures and institutions.

I believe Asian-Aryanism is neither left or right wing. But the alt-left would be in favor of letting Asian-Aryanism happen, whatever name it may take in the coming Eurasian-anime future.

8-28-17

After The Blank Banshee Show

I brought my date to Blank Banshee in Philadelphia. A friend invited me to go to the event a month in advance. I could cared less about the silly "vaporware" genre. Already, I have seen Oneohtrix Point Never live, and thought it sounded like bland digital hardcore (and not the good Atari Teenage Riot kind). I am not a fan of vaporware. I really do hate Macintosh Plus and the gay internet memes I see everywhere trying to act all "old," "ironically authentic," "Italo," or just plain stupid retro-wave shit. It is definitely a fad among millennials, like remembering every single episode of Hey Arnold! or Oh Yeah! Cartoons. However, I was in for a surprise when Blank Banshee performed live.

I have not listened to his music before. I knew he was an originator of "vaportrap," which I thought would be some gay rap music with the shit that's going around online. Again, I was wrong. I experienced an amazing movie of some sort accompanied with his music. Banshee had an MPC controller hooked up to his MacBook along with an interface and a mixer. He was pressing (or triggering) samples along a beat. He sampled old Windows 95 boot-up sounds, Sonic 3D Blast, and kitsch nostalgic noises of the 80's generation. "Postmodernism" is a disease among the Gen-X generation, and it is unfortunate if a pseudo intellect would classify Blank Banshee's music as "postmodern." But rather, he is only a part of a tradition of avant-garde musicians that sample and take what is in the era we are living through. This was the original point of "industrial" music. The same can be said about Death in June, who uses right-wing imagery and flirts with it, creating beautiful, collage art. And this is exactly what Blank Banshee is doing in the modern era.

I felt more like I was watching a movie than participating in a concert. There was no moshing, sing-a-longs, or bobbing of any sorts (hipsters try to do these things, but it has become a pastime for white people to just stand at concerts). The movie had a different scene for each song, though it felt like it was one big song and there was no end. It was like watching a rock opera with a plot and resolution. Blank Banshee could of been trying to advocate a secret political message behind his work. Such subliminal messages about love, "overcoming darkness," "teenagers buying banned music," and "chaos inside," along with references from Akira to a very strange Pokemon everyone forgot about. It's hard to pass the music as just stoner rock. Blank Banshee was rather a maestro conducting a post-millennial orchestra. Something in the tradition of the film *Imaginarium.*

The audience was unfortunately all white hipsters living in Fishtown (the most obnoxious and SWPL part of Philly). There was only ONE WMAF couple there. A cute pigtail Asian rocking out and filming the entire set (she was a little too animated). The other asian girl was some small quirky girl in overalls coming along with her friend. I cannot really claim the event as Asian-Aryan, but certainly, Blank Banshee is hitting on something.

With all the ironic hiragana floating in his music and Japanese influence, it's hard to ignore the fact he is envisioning an Asian-Aryan society. Yes, white people really do enjoy technology and growing up in this materialistic America... but Banshee was trying to say something about our culture. I thought maybe he was just a drummer to a band that will become the next Erasure or Depeche Mode... I even had the thought that if Tila Tequila was his singer, Blank Banshee would be much more revolutionary in pop music.

It was a surprise for me that I really enjoyed Blank Banshee. I'm not going to call him a simple "vaporware" or "vaportrap" act. He is tapping into something that has potential in the future. If Counter-Currents publishes books about avant-garde white nationalism and is advocating a controversial movement called the "alt-right," Blank Banshee is planting the seeds of something that is beyond left or right wing. I could see the vaporware movement involving into its own philosophy about life, art, and aesthetics. In 2030, a publishing company (something like Counter-Currents, Feral House, or Nine-Banded Books) will appear, exclusively discussing post-vaporware aesthetics, fiction, commentary, and philosophy.

The alt-right exploded because of the suppression of the political right and PC tyranny. Just like a stock making profit in the market, "alt-vapor" could have a future impact onto society. What is underground today, will have popularity in the future.

The seeds I am planting is "Asian-Aryanism." …
Something that is post-vaporware will cash in on it. Blank
Banshee and I are on different roads that will lead to one
destination.

11-3-17

The Orientals Guide to Sex, Strength, and Satisfaction

There is a coming crisis with the western (and globalized) dominant ideology of multiculturalism. The ideology is practiced among the global elites. Ironically, the white people who partake in this practice, use the religion as a "code of ethics" and a way for social signaling that they are good people.

Not only is there a strong trend of low birth rates among whites, there is also a rising population of nonwhites. If "abolishing whiteness," is the key to happiness, then why have such philosophies as capitalism, egalitarianism, Christianity, and universalism so widely spread to other nonwhites?

We could have a huge digression about the falling nature of the past three generations of white people, or how white people are pathologically altruistic, or how there is an inner nature for white people to create a futuristic transhumanist society. But I would rather spend the time discussing the importance of Larsen Helleck's book *The Orientals Guide to Sex Strength Satisfaction.*

White people today try so hard to make the multicultural system work. This requires assimilating nonwhites into white culture, or peacefully "coexisting" with them in free-market capitalism (ironically made for white people).

Radical white people are told to race-mix and create a new race of people that Richard von Coudenhove-Kalergi once dreamed of.

Unfortunately, after half a century of civil rights, nonwhites continue to separate, the white birthrate declines, and race-mixed children end up choosing a nonwhite side or committing suicide. Sadly, there is no "third-position" race that white liberals magically present (because they secretly would rather be with white liberals like themselves).

An entire generation of racially-confused, half-white people are told by white liberals that "there is no such thing as race" and "talking about such issues leads to racism." And every single half-white person should be fighting for an egalitarian society. Again, there is no third position.

The entire millennial generation of white people are waking up to this horrible Conradian horror. Deep down, they know all of this is not true. It's just Christian optimism mixed with decadent and materialistic nihilism. Another way of saying, "your life is special, now leave me alone and let me live my anime lifestyle!"

If half-whites are to follow such folly as the previous generations of whites did, then they will follow the same nihilistic death as well.

There is a question we should be confronting, "can biculturalism really work?"

We are told multiculturalism works, but we see it is a source of tension and conflict, and continues to make people separate (diehard multiculturalist should move to Brazil).

And what about the half-white people that are functioning in society? Should they just leave and go find their roots on the other side? Or are they white? I believe that neither side will accept them, and must embrace a third position where biculturalism is a functioning system. This is a crucial issue for any mixed-race person to confront. Either live or die.

...and this is where Helleck's book comes in.

Oriental Guide is written in the classic tradition of a manosphere do-it-yourself style. It is straight forward without any hidden messages. It is a manual for the dispossessed Asian American man looking for purpose.

As a disclaimer, I am not Asian. Paranoid and pretentious scholars would scoff at me saying that I am "whitesplaining" to a demographic I am ignorant of. I don't have to explain myself, since I am writing about biculturalism rather than the perspective of an Asian American.

In a race realist society, Asian men living in a white society are contested with white standards. The Asian woman falls down to the powers of the nature-breaking and romantic white men, and the obedient Asian men have to double down competition to win their own Asian American women over. This causes an extreme complication in an equality loving, liberal narrative white society. The answer for normies is to blame white men, shout for equality, or bring down strong men to weak standards. Still, it doesn't work. It causes more decadence and eventually, Asian-Aryanism.

Honest people know the truth. And Helleck gives the truth to young Asian men.

The first chapter of the book is the most significant. Helleck's thesis is that Asian men have the upmost masculine power in the world. The problem is that a growing population, globalization, and Western intervention has slowed down their true powers. There is a dragon that sleeps in every Asian man, willing to break out.

Helleck's book is manual to the let the dragon out. He provides quick arguments and refutations against liberal claims that Asians are an "oppressed" group. Going forward, Helleck provides 70 plus pages how to work out and get fit. The next few chapters are crash courses through fashion, language, and sex.

167

The reader should put down the book after reading the first 80 pages, and make up his mind if he wants to continue being disciplined. The workout routine will have a strong influence on the reader, that is, if the reader is willing to commit the time to it. In a way, the book is three books in one, but for Asian men. Imagine Arron Cleary's *Bachelor Pads Economics*, Jack Donovan's *The Way of Men*, and Roosh V's *Bang* condensed just for the Asian audience. It is very effective for the first time reader.

I would recommend to commit to Helleck's routines after reading the first and last chapter. A critical motivation must be developed before the reader goes on his intellectual journey into manhood. The reason behind the book can be summed up in 20 pages... Asian men need guidance more than ever in a failing, multicultural world.

White liberals are committing suicide, and China might as well take over America and put it in a wax museum. If any responsibility is to be accomplished, Asian-Americans must choose a side. Will they fight for their "Asian" side, or will they create something entirely new after the kali yuga? Both might happen at the same time.

Young white millennials have been trying to do the same. However, those who are race-mixed still suffer from their deluded parents and the liberal media. This is the most important group that Helleck's book can target.

Although I am pessimistic, I can be optimistic about the future. Imagine a world where human bio-diversity reigns supreme, technological advances are made in outer space, and people live in harmony with their own families. ...But where do the racially mixed people belong?

Fighting for their own side!

This book is important for the dissident niche against the modern world. I suggest you read it.

11-27-17

The Amnesty Argument

The argument which all White nationalists subscribe to is a one against race mixing. The far-right will often believe that there can be no bicultural or "third position" race. The argument follows that there can be only "White" or "Asian." There simply cannot be a "Eurasian" one. The mixed race person (or something that isn't mixed at all) must choose a team consisting of either red or blue. There is no purple team.

Greg Johnson of Counter-Currents will also extend the argument to include "people of some mixed Asian ancestry" in an all-white ethnostate. But that person cannot ultimately race mix further. This is an amnesty. There is amnesty for mixed race people and they have to choose a side. Hence I call this phenomenon the "amnesty argument."

Debate or talk to anyone on the alt-right, and the argument is that mixed race people belong on THAT side, but not the white one. In a way, there is a society of high minded white aristocrat, and then a sweeping mass of brown degenerate people. How has this citation improved?

White nationalist claim to have truth on their side. But the actual truth is, they don't have an answer for the other, simply because they don't care about the other. Hipster racism has already infiltrated the alt-right, creating more plants like Lauren Rose and Tara McCarthy.

The Golden One explained in a video (I forget which one) that what the Cultural Marxist did to academia in 60s, is what the Alt-right will do in 2020. There is now Cultural Fascism. No one wants to debate it because it is the hip and edgy norm all the cool kids are gravitating towards. They take their ideology from already established white nationalist and reinvent for their poorly thought out high-school mentality of social signaling.

White millennials are being proselytized to become white nationalist, and will neglect the future for half-white people. Do these mixed people assert themselves as fellow white people? Or do they belong in the gas chamber? There is no answer.

I, however, assert that biculturalism is the answer. And for Whites and Asians, call it "Eurasianism" or "Asian Aryanism."

In a future where neo-liberalism is doomed, ethnonationalism will eventually replace it. And when ethnonationalism does replace the PC-tyrannical Kalergi plan, ethnonationalism will advocate that all races belong back to their designated "homelands." Basically, Zionism for all peoples.

If ethnonationalsim was to reach out to a larger audience, then it should be reach out to those who don't belong to a 100% "white" or "Asian" side. There has to be an institution that advocates biculturalism. Such a place would be the size of an Amish community. It could be in an white or Asian ethnosate, but have its own control (like Taiwan). Could such a place be envisioned?

This is what I have been arguing for. The Amnesty Argument is not enough to answer the events of the past century. We simply cannot forget past history and move forward. There is no white-nationalist janitor that cleans out the decadence of the past and everything is wonderfully fixed. Technology is growing, and will eliminate certain generation social norms and trends.

Transhumanism is an opponent against white nationalism. Asian-Aryanism is not transhumanist, but is ethnonationalist and bicultural. This a problem the alt-right must face, but clearly it is too busy watching and consuming Youtube drama.

The normie doesn't want the arts. The normie wants to norm but also wants to be an individual. The alt-right is a collective party of white individuals who want to believe they are in a collective. A sad high school mentality that addresses nothing.

In the end, international capitalism will make profit off the alt-rights demands, and they will always be keyboard warriors consuming and being complacent. Like someone who watches info wars.

Normies hate eccentrics because they don't understand them. They want the alt-right to control crazy behavior. The world would be simple if people were just red or blue. If only the truth was grounded on the reality of race and sexuality, things would be better.

But no one on the alt-right has an answer for the differences of race or sexuality. They claim it, and watch as they suck into the powers of Lauren Rose and admire anime.

This dangerous belief of "claiming to be based on the truth" is what motivates arrogance in the normie looking for attention.

Jim Goad, who is an ultimate skeptic and truth seeker, is not someone on the alt-right. He does his own thing. And does a good job at it. I would classify myself as a Goadian. It doesn't mean I have to subscribe to a new world religion based upon ethnonationalism. What it means is that I fight against the hypocrisy of normal people, because quite frankly, I hate normies. I hate when normies try and disguise themselves to be like me, do I find them to be even more repulsive.

The amnesty argument is a one-dimensional argument for ideological normies. They don't have answers. Just social signals. *12-24-17*

Truth and Fantasy

If you read a white nationalist publication like counter-currents, often the argument is that they are providing the "truth" on their side. This truth is based upon objective and grounded reality. This can range from race studies, classical philosophy, and *The Bell Curve*.

What makes white nationalism and the Alt-Right so appealing to our generation, is not only that it is anti-liberal in nature, but it offers Sargon-of-Akkad-tier arguments for the truth which millennials have been fogged over by the boomers. Once someone goes 1488, they can never switch back over to a Marxist ideology. Why is that? Because truth is on the white nationalist side.

Marxist have created a utopian dream society that can only be realized through social engineering and propaganda. In other words, there is a trans humanist war against the natural world. Marxists are rebelling against mother nature, and ethnonationalists are trying to find commune within nature (creating a "human bio-diversity" future and Martin Heidegger style socialism).

This spiritual war is between two parties. Yet, the argument is twofold. Ethnonationalists believe you should come to their side because they have the truth, while Marxist believe we should fight against all forms of oppression and create the selfish society we want to live in as individuals.

174

…Both unfortunately seem to be wrong.

Marxists are wrong for many reasons, but white nationalists are wrong for assuming radical honesty is the answer. There is nothing wrong with being honest. In fact, I hate people who are inauthentic and hypocritical, even those who show one drop of it. What white nationalists do not understand is that youth is a motivator for truth.

Often drug-addicted and perverted nazis will say that "youth is a folly and everything I learned from my cultural Marxist professors was wrong. If only I had been more 'based' and became a Traditionalist I would have found greater meaning in life." Millennials, now hitting their mid 20s, are going through something similar.

Liberals tend to call this "woke," while the Alt-Right says its taking the "red pill." (Personally, I believe these coming-to-age terminologies are postmodern in nature and divide the individual with irony and eclecticism). Youth was only a "phase" for them and nothing special. It was the loss of innocence handed over to guilt created the complex scientist-playing-god adult. Right?

I am very skeptical (and have intense hatred) for the individual who claims they are an "adult" now. (Because they drink beer, smoke cigarettes, work a full-tine job, use tinder for inane and disgusting one night stands, do drugs at "parties," swear like a sailor, while upholding that they are someone the descendent of Socrates).

Religion has proven throughout time that humanity needs to build civilization in order to go forward. That means morals and ethics must be enforced. A true man against the kali yuga role-plays the Christ figure. Someone must become a martyr in order to show this decadent world there is hope in humanity. I am strong advocate of Rene Girard's philosophy.

"Adultism" runs rampant in society by those who are irresponsible. "When you're 30, you will realize there is more to life than partying!" (ironically said by someone who did those same things), and "I am 22 years old and I can work at Apple!" (said by someone who lacks experience and is full of arrogance).

Life is an ongoing journey through wisdom and knowledge, and any healthy human being should grow, not die, as they age. Faulty conclusions are reached at certain points, such as the The Asian Feminist Fallacy. Or that the adult is still a kid trapped inside a grown-up body. It should be a priority for every human being to contribute towards society and create a greater civilization for future generations.

...But all of this I have just written... is any of it grounded in "truth?" It sounds like it. But what if one does something different to achieve a greater society, like through Asian-

Aryanism or Marxism? A white nationalist would argue that both are living in a dream bubble. That a magazine like Cosmopolitan sells dreams. And now pornography controls our sexuality.

In 2017, we live in a society behind computer screens and communicate writing digital letters. We use virtual avatars to represent ourselves and play video games for fun. The outside world is becoming bleak and darker, as the white people who consume in this technology run away from the nature of the world. Technology progresses and the population is booming. The western world is becoming "Asianized."

All of this is a fantasy, yet in practical terms, it is becoming a reality. White nationalists argue that by reversing such trends, whites could find the Heidegger-style "truth" and make rational, Christian choice. White men would then choose white women simply because "it's for the greater good." Again, where is this greater good if everyone is already enjoying watching anime and watching Lauren Rose videos?

For all the white people that end up reproducing with other white people, they will have to grow another generation of "racially aware" whites, preferring them over the seething masses of nonwhites. (maybe something like The Node will happen). This hyper-conscious attempt to uphold society is based upon anxiety and racial duty. And white nationalism will continue to argue that it is based upon the "truth." In

177

other words, if you can imagine the philosophy of Martin Heidegger becoming a movement, it would be ethnonationalism.

That is not to say Martin Heidegger is wrong. But the radical attempts to try and box people away from their own freedom of association is wrong. White people have an amazing trait to go beyond the limit of mother nature, and in doing so, they wish to create something much greater in life. White people have created rockets to the moon and modern forms of art.

In a bleak world full of nonwhites, white people will not be there to create the progressing future. It's why I subscribe to ethnonationalism. But at the same time, ultimately, I am a eurasian futurist. I am an anti-liberal at heart trying to find the right system that will cause the least conflict and make every person on earth happy.

A communist country can exist over there, and a Spencer all-white-utopia down there. But I would like to live in that hip place over there, that has all the whites, Asians, and Eurasians living together in harmony. That is ethnonationalism in a nutshell.

And still, there are Nazis who claim that any form of coexistence and biculturalism is wrong and not based upon "truth." If they had it their way, they would eliminate the future possibility of a bicultural or mixed-race person. Either they are "red" or they are "blue."

Truth does exist. We often have fantasies about our future. We can make our dreams become a reality if we work hard to achieve them. Most normies live in fantasies they learn from watching television and browsing the internet. Obviously if someone is "gay," 30% of the country must be gay too! And if Enid from *OK KO: Let's Be Friends* is a black, purple haired ninja girl, well, there must be a person like her in this world.

René Girard argued that life is about the mimic throes. People desire what other people want. "If he has an Asian girlfriend, then I want an Asian girlfriend too!"

Is it bad life is based upon envy, jealously, and dreams to escape reality? There are negative consequences that a smart person must realize in order to overcome. But desires don't change.

I know too many white nationalists that once had Asian girlfriends in their youth (and had sex with them), only then to "grow up" and say "I'm into traditionalist white girls now and the alt-right is the future." This is a great example of hypocrisy, inauthenticity, and stupidity.

People who do this are denying their true nature. They are running away from their true desires of life to pursue

179

something that is artificial and not them. As Girard puts it, they take the life of someone else. Other symptoms, like depressions and lack of confidence might be a motivator of this action. But ultimately, I strongly believe it has to do with stupidity, adults, and true immaturity.

And these same people will tell you "truth" is on their side. Mind you, it's a trick for hipster racism. Watch out. Realize its they who are misguided in life and sin by becoming too "edgy" for preening purposes.

If there was any truth to this, they want life to become like an anime.

The argument they make is the same Ryan Anderson makes in *The Birth of Prudence*. "Well, it has nothing to do with the fact that she is Asian, but, choosing white over Asian is the right thing to do." I also assume Ryan is guilty of Asian-sexual desires. But he doubles down and pretends he's doing the "right" thing. Why would you write a book in the first place?

To refute Asian-Aryanism? No. It's about himself. This "truth" veneer is quite dangerous for most young people. It denies their desires and gives into "truth-nihilism." A bleak system of "well it doesn't accord with white nationalism, so I can't truly respect this piece of art."

Millennials are trying so hard to be unique. But in the end, they are still snowflakes. Just like me.

12-24-17

Fashwave Sectarianism Vs. Vaporwave Hegemony

In a recent liberal hit piece,[16] fashwave was called "the suicidal retro-futurist art of the alt-right." We are warned that this fringe art movement is proselytizing young people into a racist movement full of "hate." The article presents the fashwave phenomenon as another mischievous creation of the far-Right, hijacking a popular genre, vaporwave, for its political aims. As Jack Smith writes, "vaporwave is set up perfectly for a right-wing heist, just as the far right has stolen leftist youth culture for decades, from Hitler to heavy metal."

As if the only type of art we will ever have comes from the Left.

It is only natural for popular art to filter into all forms of intellectual discourse. And when chan culture, ruled by an order of isolated and socially inept young people, creates memes and clashes with the normie class, one such result is fashwave.

But a better understanding of fashwave should not come from *why* and *what* makes it popular, but *where* all this original art is coming from.

Vaporwave is one of the most significant and influential artistic movements of the last decade. You've seen memes

---

16 https://mic.com/articles/187379/this-is-fashwave-the-suicidal-retro-futurist-art-of-the-alt-right

where "A E S E T H I C" is spelled out as if written by a Japanese person. And you might have seen Greek busts of Helios and bubblegum pink tiles too. It's all a function of the outsize influence of a "micro-genre" of music: vaporwave.

Music genres propagate and ramify like internet memes. But such micro-genres as seapunk, chillwave, witch house, and cloud rap all come from one original source, and that is vaporwave.

Vaporwave is a genre of electronic music that pays tribute to the music of the 1980s, 1990s, and earlier decades of nostalgic-tech and media.

Smith declares that fashwave is problematic for the globalist project: "Vaporwave and fashwave both play in the ruins of modern consumerism. And both genres force us to consider how much we have lost so quickly."

Why is there such an End-of-the-World slant to vaporwave?

The first ever vaporwave release was Daniel Lopatin's *Chuck Pearson's Eccojams Vol. 1*. This was a humorous release of cut-up or "plunderphonic" samples of cheesy pop songs. "Ecco" was a reference to the Sega Genesis game of the same name (many millennials grew up playing the game or knowing about it).

Lopatin's ethnic background is Russian and Jewish. He cites Deleuze, DeLanda, and Heidegger as philosophical influences. Typical of his postmodern upbringing, often Lopatin creates avant-garde, "guggenheim" style of electronic music under the name Oneohtrix Point Never. *Eccojams* has since became an early *magnum opus* in his career and in vaporwave. As Lopatin has stated in an interview:

> *"I remember reading this great philosopher named Julia Kristeva, a French feminist philosopher, and she says — generally, she says a lot of amazing things — but in this essay called "Powers of Horror" she talks about the abject things that come out that we have desire to see. So the things that we try to contain within us is like this pre-semiotic reality and society is the way we want to present ourselves. Like, we wear clothes, and things are not coming out, there's no excrement or whatever."* 17

Lopatin feels a certain attitude of deracination towards everything (a term of praise for a postmodern philosopher). It is very common in the vaporwave genre to express feelings of consumer nihilism. And often this flirtation with so-called cutting-edge postmodern philosophy makes everything more pretentious.

Another important release to come out of the vaporwave canon was Mactintosh Plus's *Floral Shoppe*. Its iconic album art, featuring that Greek bust, has become staple for all jokes about vaporwave. It was also the primary influence on the emergence of fashwave.

---

17 https://www.theverge.com/2015/11/12/9723304/ oneohtrix-point-never-daniel-lopatin-interview-garden-of-delete

However, the album's creator goes by the name "Ramona Andra Xavier," a non-cisgendered person of color. Xavier was also in email contact with Lopatin, making this social connection all too conspiratorial.

In a popular YouTube documentary about the history of vaporwave, the narrator, Wolfenstien OS X, defines the fall of vaporwave after the adoption of the *Floral Shoppe* consumer ideology it promoted (6:40):

"This ideal for the genre continue to dominate the tone of most vaporwave releases... This gave the genre a bad rap as it seemed to be stagnant in its development and was doomed to be an awkward phase of music, which was shallow in meaning and production quality. Eventually most releases were horribly put together messes just to undermine the true essence of what of the genre was about." [18]

Traditionally, vaporwave was "hyponagogic," meaning that the music was to evoke a dreamlike state and certain feelings of nostalgia in the listener. This is why often vaporwave releases are slowed-down versions popular songs, creating an otherworldly muzak. The genre took other names like "mall-soft," or the rave style of "hardvapour." This is what retro-wave music also does, as it feeds into nostalgia for 1980s synthpop.

It is very popular for vaporwave to be exclusively released on cassette tapes. Bandcamp.com has outsourced the entire genre through their website. Cassette runs are often limited

[18] https://www.youtube.com/watch?v=PdpP0mXOlWM

185

to 30-60 copies and fetch high prices on Discogs and Ebay. Vaporwave dared to challenge the market of cassette culture by creating a genre of music that resembles nostalgic artifacts. Rather, as Wolfenstein OS X explains, it is "post-music," and the genre is not to be casually listened to like "music," but to be enjoyed for the fact of its own existence. Popular vaporwave cassettes are judged and sold on the fact that it gives the listener feelings of escapism.

There is even an *essential guide to vaporwave*,[19] which is a good introduction to the genre. Not all of the music is good. In fact, most of it is bad. There are probably two or three albums you will admire from the list. I strongly believe the purpose of this guide and Wolfenstein OS X's vaporwave documentary was to sell more cassettes from the Dream Catalogue label.

I believe that vaporwave is inherently reactionary, because it is nostalgic. But there is also something decadent about vaporwave. Music is being solely created as pretty pieces of artwork. Everything is alienated, and nothing meaningful is being established. Postmodern philosophy is running rampant, while SWPL hipsters use its logic to justify the genre. And ever since *Eccojams*, this formula has been regurgitating in the Bandcamp marketplace. It is an anonymous 4chan culture of "post-music" that has no greater meaning. This is the globalist agenda of vaporwave. It only wants you to buy more cassettes from Bandcamp while pretending you are an expert on Deleuze.

---

[19] Google search it.

186

The genre of vaporwave has become a tool for chan culture, and thus it was only natural for *The Daily Stormer* trolls to take advantage of it. Thus, fashwave was created to instill meaning back into the vaporwave movement.

Fashwave's most important acts are Xurious and Cybernazi. Both Xurious and Cybernazi typically create retro-futuristic, italo-disco-style music that differs from the hypnogogic style of releases of *Eccojams* and *Floral Shoppe.*

Xurious has played at NPI and conceives his target audience as the Alt Right. Cybernazi does the same thing, but remains anonymous over the internet. Fashwave is stuck in the Right-wing ghetto, as it became solely a vaporwave "cultural appropriation" for the Alt Right. I understand Right-wing genres of music can embrace everyone from Death In June and Peste Noire to Taylor Swift. The similarity is that these acts all openly or implicitly touch upon our people and our interests.

Since most of the Alt Right movement listens to Xurious, Cybernazi, and horrible "Weird Al" Yankovic neo-nazi dubs of pop songs, it's a mistake to think fashwave is an up and coming music genre. It will soon die in its right-wing ghetto, until a new popular music genre will appear. And then the far-Right will appropriate that new genre for its audience, leading to another liberal hit piece.

But fashwave is just too good to confine itself to the Right-wing ghetto. To make a real impact on the culture, fashwave must adopt a "today the Alt Right, tomorrow the world" ethos. We have to make fashwave global.

The way forward has been blazed by Blank Banshee. If there is one major vaporwave act that is influencing music today that a healthy Right-wing person could like, my suggestion is Blank Banshee.

Blank Banshee is targeting inner-city hipsters and a majority of people who are just discovering vaporwave. Blank Banshee, or Patrick Driscoll, is an authoritative figure of post-vaporwave. Oneohtrix Point Never is too busy creating globalist friendly artsy music, and Vektroid is too arrogant, chasing after "scene" credibility.

Blank Banshee came into the genre as the first "vapor trap" act. That is a mix between vaporwave and trap music. His debut album, *0*, was a viral meme and snowballed the success of his music career.

But perhaps Blank Banshee's most loved album is *1*, his second album. On the album, "Ecozones" is a tribute to Donkey Kong Country's Aquatic Ambience. "Anxiety Online," "LSD Polyphony," "Big Gulp," and "Cyber Slums" are some of the best vaporwave dance songs ever released. But tracks like "Doldrum Corp," "Realization," and "Paradise Disc," bring about a certain aesthetic dream vision, more than what fashwave has tried to impose. What makes this album stand out are the CGI visuals that accompany the songs during live performance. It is very difficult for any artist to create such a *Gesamtkunstwerk*.

It is assumed that Blank Banshee created all the visuals to go along with the release. He is also said to have released some CD-Rs in the Chinese black market (this might be a joke). He shares a penchant for anonymity with another electronic act, Boards of Canada. Boards of Canada is known for avoiding all interviews and giving little information about their releases, yet they have a giant fan base, including a Fox News reporter. Blank Banshee wears a mask like Death in June and hides from all public interviews. His live performances include a giant movie projector of his animations, as he triggers samples from his MPC controller. His music ranges from sample snippets of video games to anime, from *Super Mario 64* to *Akira*, with lush and atmospheric hip-hop beats and textures. It supersedes the boring mall muzak of *Eccojams* and approaches a new form of pop music that truly envisions a new future.

Blank Banshee has released all of his albums on cassette, which quickly sold out during the Christmas season of 2017. His debut 2017 tour was very promising as it was the first major "vaporwave" act to tour the United States and Canada.

Blank Banshee does not align his music with any political ideology and is quite playful with his art. It is hard to admire something that is egalitarian and Marxist or the creeping postmodern message that is trying to latch onto vaporwave. But listening to fashwave, just because it is "fashy," is stubborn and self-defeating.

At its core, the vaporwave genre nostalgically admires the past: VHS tapes, electronic synthesizers, retro-futuristic

189

cars, vector grids, vintage arcade games, bad consumer products, Japanese culture, etc. Subverting it with fascist imagery is not enough. Death in June is a master at this collage art. Let's just leave it to him.

Vaporwave is the music of the future. If vaporwave is inherently reactionary, nostalgic, and retro-futurist, it is *already* Right-wing. The *whole* thing is Right-wing. Not just the fashwave secession. What I would like to see is a critical discourse that accompanies and interprets the vaporwave genre as an essentially *anti-liberal* art form sprung from a *sincere* longing for the future we were promised but denied, without cutting itself on edgy National Socialist and Evola memes. Sure, people will try to trot out *Capitalism and Schizophrenia*, but it's up to us to call out such errors in thinking. It is up to us to construct a dominant anti-liberal paradigm to eventually turn vaporwave discourse, and the music itself, against the globalist nihilism and transhumanist philosophy

of *Eccojams* and *Floral Shoppe*.

Fashwave is dead! Long live fashwave!

2-23-18

Queerness, Homonationalism, and Post-Liberalism

There are a few individuals in the far right that are gay. All of them are quiet about it. Milo Yiannopoulos once stood out as being the alt-right faggot. Not anymore.

Gays in the far-right are an extroverted class. No one online proclaims themselves as "the gay alt-right guy." But when you meet these guys at weirdo events, I'm sure they are happy to tell you how gay they are (and how cool it is).

Personally, I have met five closeted homos in the far-right sphere. Note: not "alt-right" scene. Right-wing gays are perhaps the most intellectual of all right-wing thinkers. It's like being a monk. Women are sexual demons, and these sensitive men are favoring the bond of intellectualism.

Alisdair Clarke was one of the only esoteric gay people in the far-right, and did a good job fighting for a new Männerbund homosexuality. I will repeat, there is an esoteric reason for being gay in the far-right.

...Death in June anyone?

But let's get to the bottom of this. You are a snowflake for being in the alt-right.

I don't want to hear how cool you are for hanging out with James Allsup, attending Unite The Right, and keeping up with the latest Murdoch Murdoch cartoons. Chances are,

191

you're a special individual. You're a typical millennial. Your life depends on being special.

And that's exactly what queerness is about.

Being "queer" does not mean having a deviant sexuality. A few decades ago, if you were some avant-garde beatnik into Ellsworth Kelly and Richard Williams, you were strange. You had feelings against the "squares" and the normative society. If only things were more about freedom of expression and complete liberalism.

The next thing you know, NAMBLA supporters, promiscuous flower children, and punk rockers all hijacked the word "queer."

Face it. You are in the alt-right because you want to be strange yourself. It's what empowers you. Your life is like a Steven Universe drama. This is the true meaning behind queerness.

Yet some have the audacity (and stubbornness) of thinking that being homosexual and associating with a movement that would literally throw them in an oven is not wrong at all.

…I know all you fags love the attention. You love this paradox. It makes your traumas more justified and your personality spicier.

Keith Haring would once plaster New York with his "Go Home Clones," graffiti, because he believed there were "clone" gays and authentic ones. He apparently believed he was the authentic one (or so he thought).

Young people are in a high-school preening contest. And all of you homonationalist want a world without globalism just to sound cool. You know that being gay is a white virtue. You don't want black cock, small Asian cock, or foreign cock that is scary (It feels like rape, I know). You want nice, ethical and charming white cock. You know if there are no more white people, there is no more gay culture. You are homosexuals that discriminate in favor of daddy rape fantasies, dressed in Nazi uniforms.

You get high off this stuff.

…But you're also an anti-liberal.

We can all agree we hate SJWs. We hate our baby boomer parents. We want a world without public education teaching about the holocaust. Yeah, yeah, yeah.

"So that is the narrative for all normies in the alt-right, isn't it?" You see, the glacier gets deeper.

The left is all about progressive stacking, that is, letting the black tranny speak first. And how ironic is it, when the new "based" gay guy will make a new progressive stacking technique for all the far-right to see. *"How about we let the cis-gendered white man speak first! Then let us cool faggots speak at a private invite-only freemason event. You wouldn't think of us as normal gay people, because we are all about making society normal in favor of protecting our own queerness!"*

Blaire White, a right-wing tranny, is only saying the things he says for fame. Just like how XXXtentacion, Lil Pump, Liluzivert, Slim Jesus, and other Soundcloud rappers get into their own drama.

Google forces us to appreciate some bizarre artist every other day on their front "Google doodle" page to make even the dumbest normie feel enlightened. Some on the esoteric far-right are hard at work trying to dig up snowflakes that have been buried in the past for being too fringy (Miguel Serrano, Savitri Devi, Julius Evola). Is this good? Or is just another hipster outlet of finding "that really good record?"

Imagine one day, in 2050, when the new elite have Camille Paglia as a Google doodle.

If the millennial generation is defined by a trait, it is that we are a generation of hipsters, whether we admit this or not. Young people only care about impressing their social peers. It's cool to be the black guy, asian girl, tranny, or gay guy in the far-right.

Oh well, Orwell! What have we gotten ourselves into?

I strongly believe that there needs to be a party for open far-right homosexuals. They have remained in closet because it is now actually "cool" to be a closet faggot again. However, it's only "cool" to let the normie white guy

194

speak, and ironically let the underground gay guys be hipsters again. Gay people always feel like outsiders (just like you, dear reader). This is the snowflake mentality.

I dare you! Take a step out of the closet and create a gay party for the far-right. Identity politics is inevitable. If human bio-diversity and the philosophy of Martin Heidegger is to flourish, then I suggest we end all white lies (pun intended). Truth lies in authenticity. Inauthentic people beat their wife and cheat on them (Matthew Heimbach).

The far-right in the coming decades will morph into cultural fascism, and all inner city hipsters will create a new "fashy" subculture. And it will be full of "poz," contradicting that the introverted alt-right hates.

We can keep our unique homonationalism, but let us admit to the fact that we are all queer people, wishing to overthrow the neoliberal elite. If you can imagine a right-wing version of *The Wild Boys: A Book of The Dead*, so be it.

3-15-18

Francis Nally (1991-) was born and raised in Pennsylvania. He graduated from Rosemont College with a degree in English and Communications. Nally wrote two books under the pen name, "pilleater," *Almond Eyes, Baby Face* (2016) and *Trip* (2017). His band is Phteven Universe and has released

four cassettes; *Phteven Universe*, おさ

かなといっしょ, *illicit*, and *Asian Girlfriend* (all released in 2018). Nally continues to blog on social media and post videos on YouTube.

www.pilleater.com https://
www.youtube.com/pilleater https://
twitter.com/realpilleater https://
www.facebook.com/pilleaters https://
www.instagram.com/pilleater https://
choamcharity.bandcamp.com http://
ytmnd.com/users/pilleater

www.ingramcontent.com/pod-product-compliance
Lightning Source LLC
Chambersburg PA
CBHW020958180626
46814CB00003B/1149